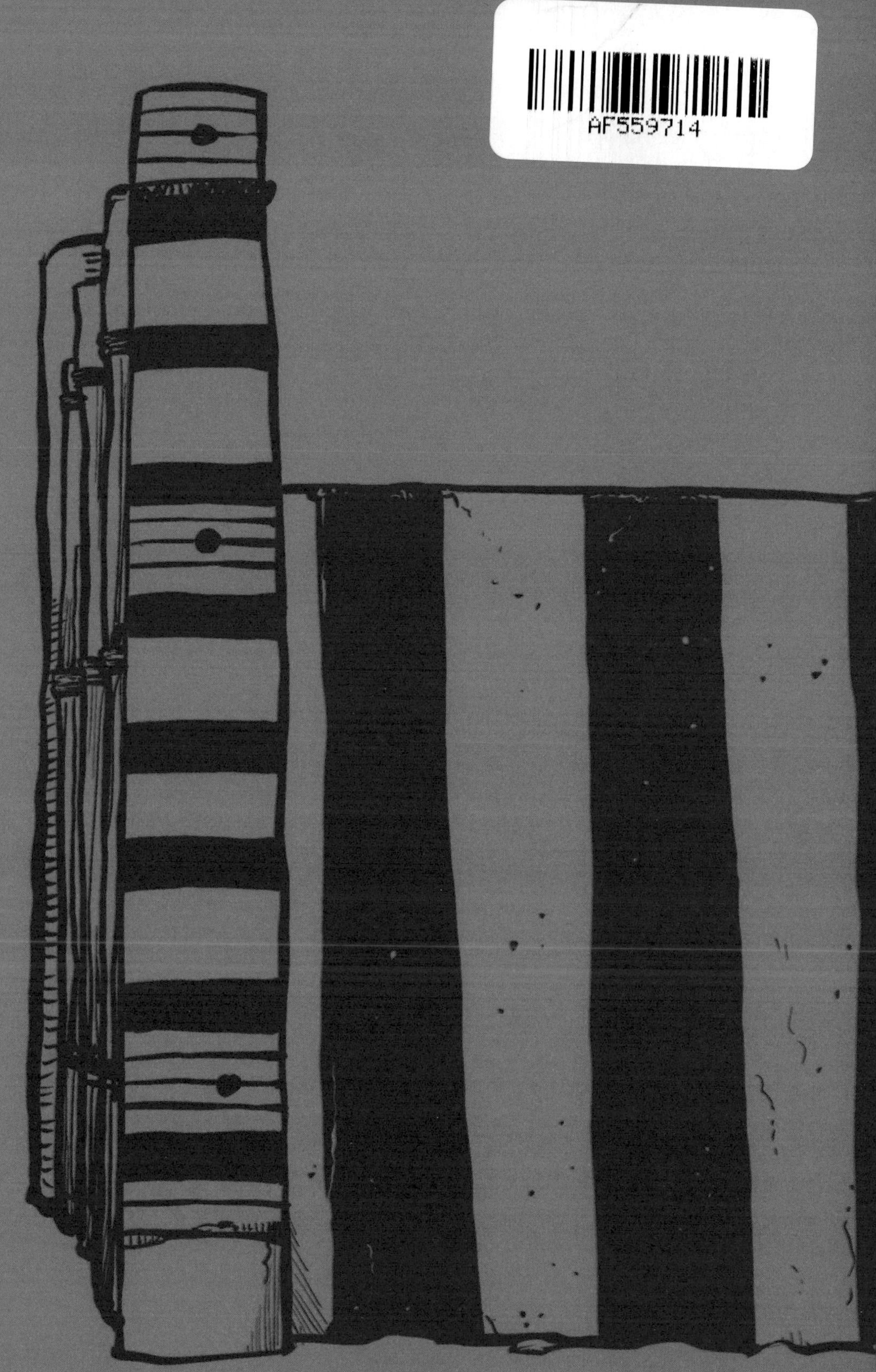

Advance praise

'Jallikattu finds mentions in Tamil history from time immemorial, but *Vaadivasal*, a short novel authored by C.S. Chellappa in the 1950s, was the first fictional work on this subject. Even now, it remains one of the most significant literary creations on this traditional cultural sport. Today, when Jallikattu is such a contested and passionate issue, this novel needs to be re-discovered. *Vaadivasal* deals not only with human and animal relationship but also goes beyond that singular frame and foregrounds the reality of social hierarchies and human psychology. The writing is so vivid and visual that it lends itself to becoming a graphic novel. The artist Appupen has brilliantly brought Chellappa's words to life and Perumal Murugan has sensitively adapted the original dialogues to suit Appupen's interpretation. It is important that the written word finds new ways of reaching people through pictorial and cinematic creativity. I am so glad that *Vaadivasal* will be seen and read by a new generation that is grappling with the very same socio-cultural questions that the novel raised more than half a century ago.'

—**T.M. Krishna,** Ramon Magsaysay awardee,
Carnatic vocalist, and author

'A story of violence, death and vengeance... by a Gandhian.'

—**Ashokamitran,** author, in *The Hindu*

C.S. Chellappa's

VAADIVAASAL

THE ARENA

SIMON &
SCHUSTER

London · New York · Sydney · Toronto · New Delhi

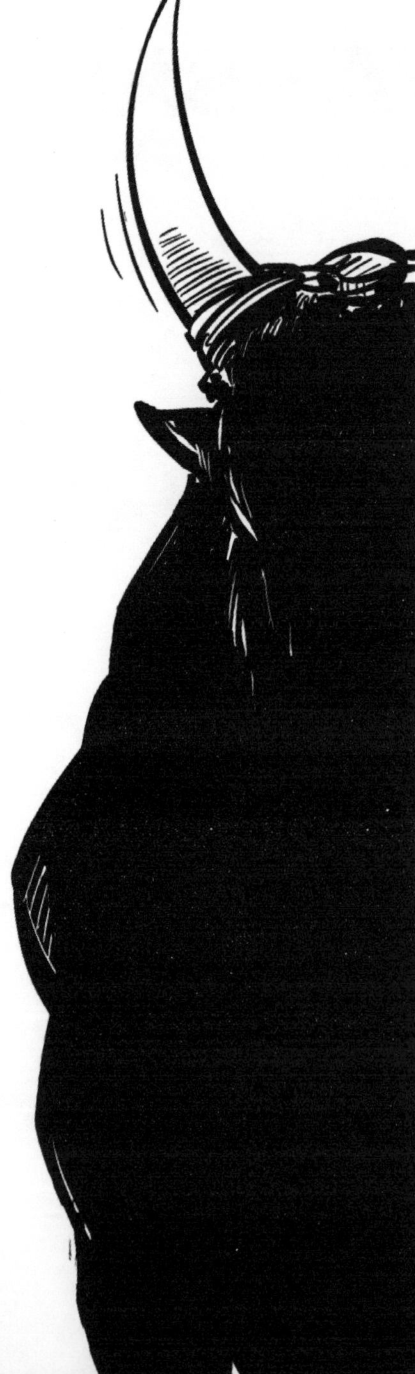

Adapted from: Vaadivaasal by C.S. Chellappa
Script: Perumal Murugan
Visualisation & art: Appupen
Layout & design: Appupen, Natasha Rego
English translation:
Kavitha Muralidharan, Appupen

First published in India by Simon & Schuster India, 2025

Published by arrangement with Kalachuvadu Publications

ISBN :
Paperback 978-81-983564-1-3
eBook 978-81-983564-7-5

1 3 5 7 9 10 8 6 4 2

Simon & Schuster India
818, Indraprakash Building,
21, Barakhamba Road,
New Delhi 110001.

www.simonandschuster.co.in

Printed and bound in India by Replika Press Pvt. Ltd.

C.S. Chellappa's

VAADIVAASAL

THE ARENA

Adapted by
Perumal Murugan & Appupen

SIMON & SCHUSTER
London · New York · Sydney · Toronto · New Delhi

CHELLAYIPURAM.

AFTERNOON.
AROUND 4PM.

PEOPLE ARE HEADING TOWARDS THE VAADIVAASAL.

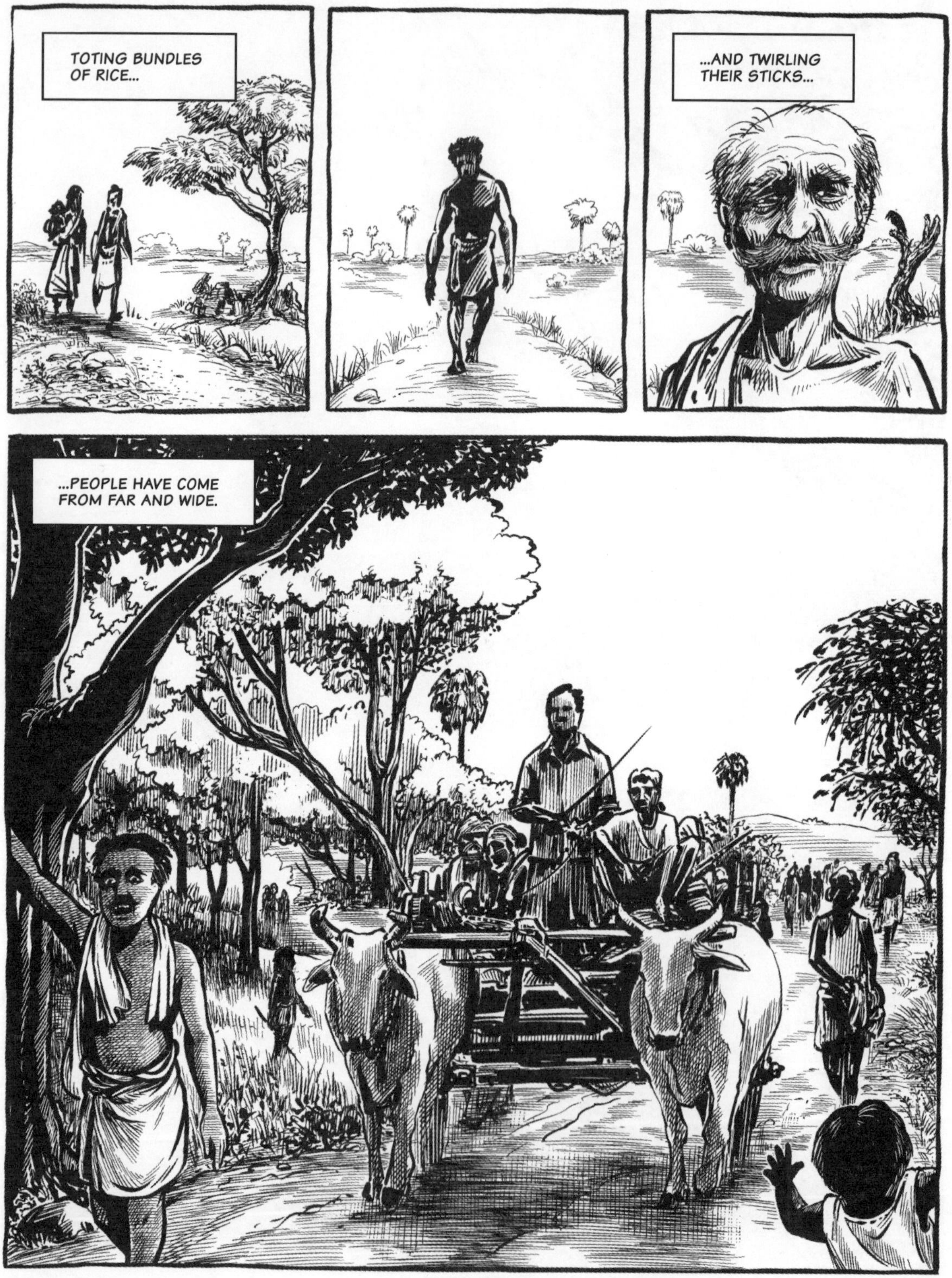

...PEOPLE HAVE COME FROM FAR AND WIDE.

THE JALLIKATTU BULLS ARE BEING LED TO THE VAADIVAASAL BY THEIR PROUD OWNERS.

THE CROWD SWELLS AT THE JALLIKATTU ARENA.
MEN AND WOMEN. EVEN CHILDREN.

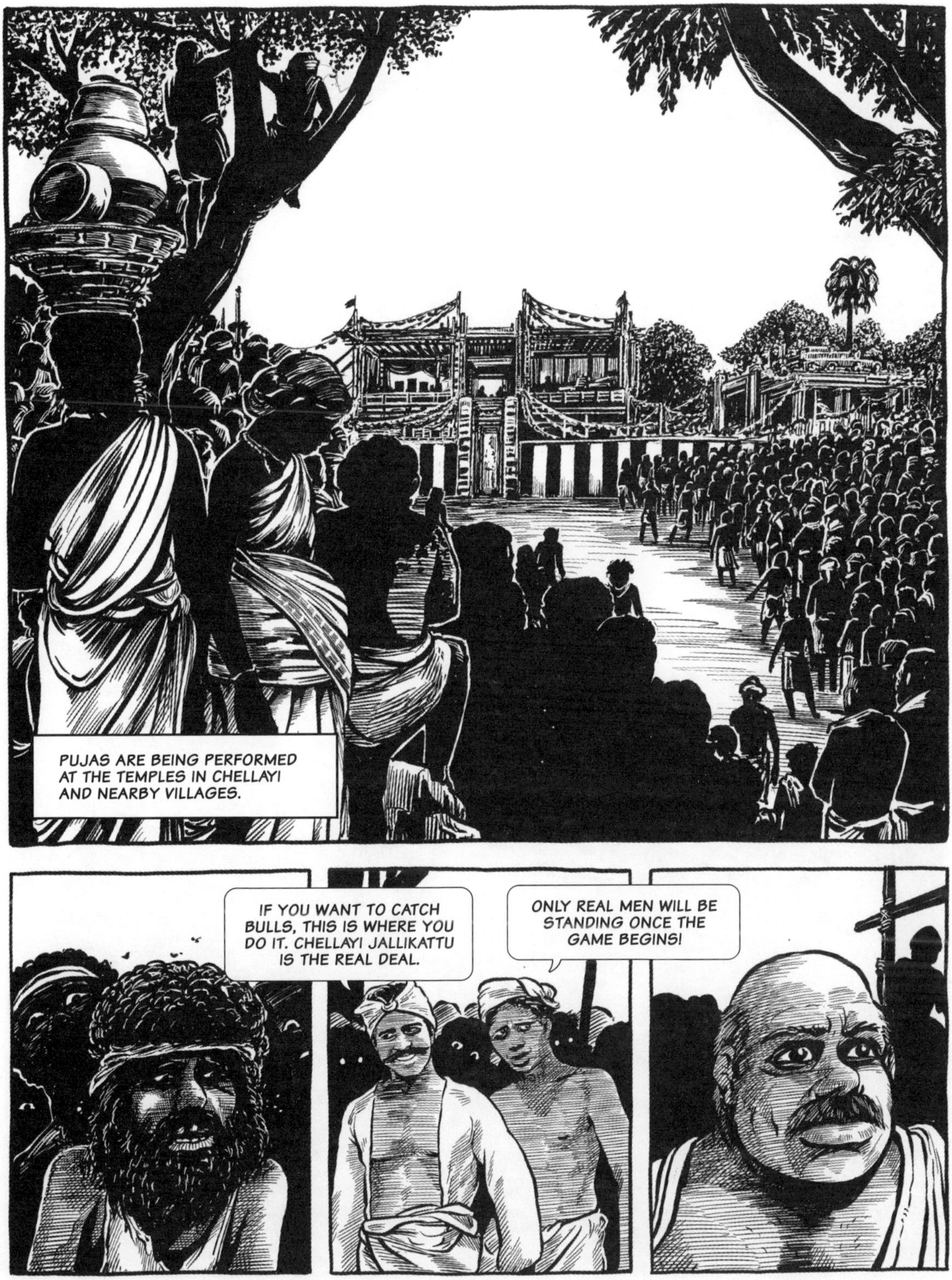

PUJAS ARE BEING PERFORMED AT THE TEMPLES IN CHELLAYI AND NEARBY VILLAGES.

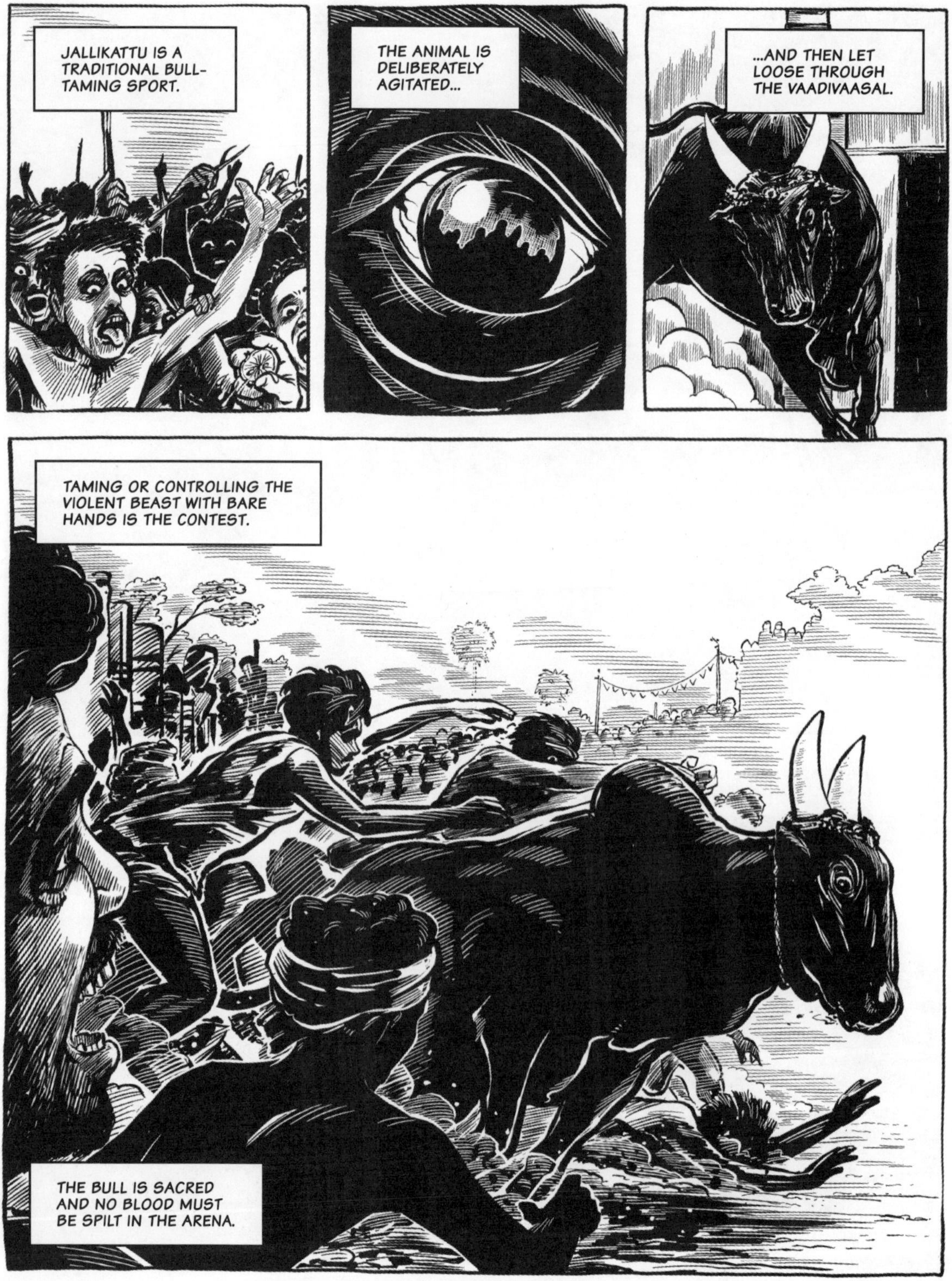

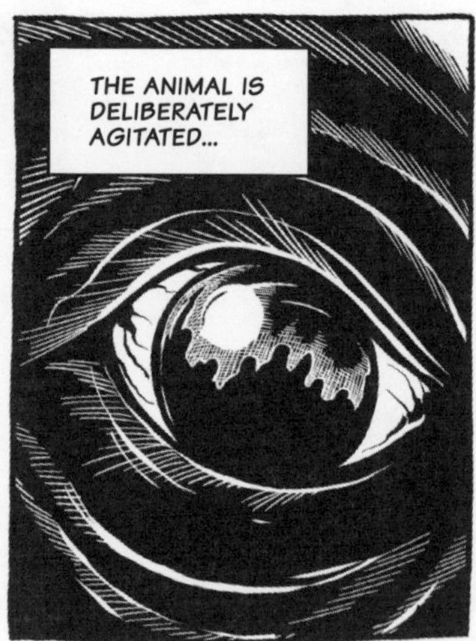

TAMING OR CONTROLLING THE VIOLENT BEAST WITH BARE HANDS IS THE CONTEST.

THE BULL IS SACRED AND NO BLOOD MUST BE SPILT IN THE ARENA.

THE TAMER CAN ONLY CATCH THE BULL BY ITS HUMP OR HORNS. AND HE MUST NOT LET GO.

TO WIN, THE TAMER MUST HOLD THE BULL STILL FOR A FEW SECONDS.

THE TAMER CAN THEN MANOEUVRE IT DOWN TO THE GROUND OR SNATCH THE REWARD HANGING BETWEEN THE HORNS.

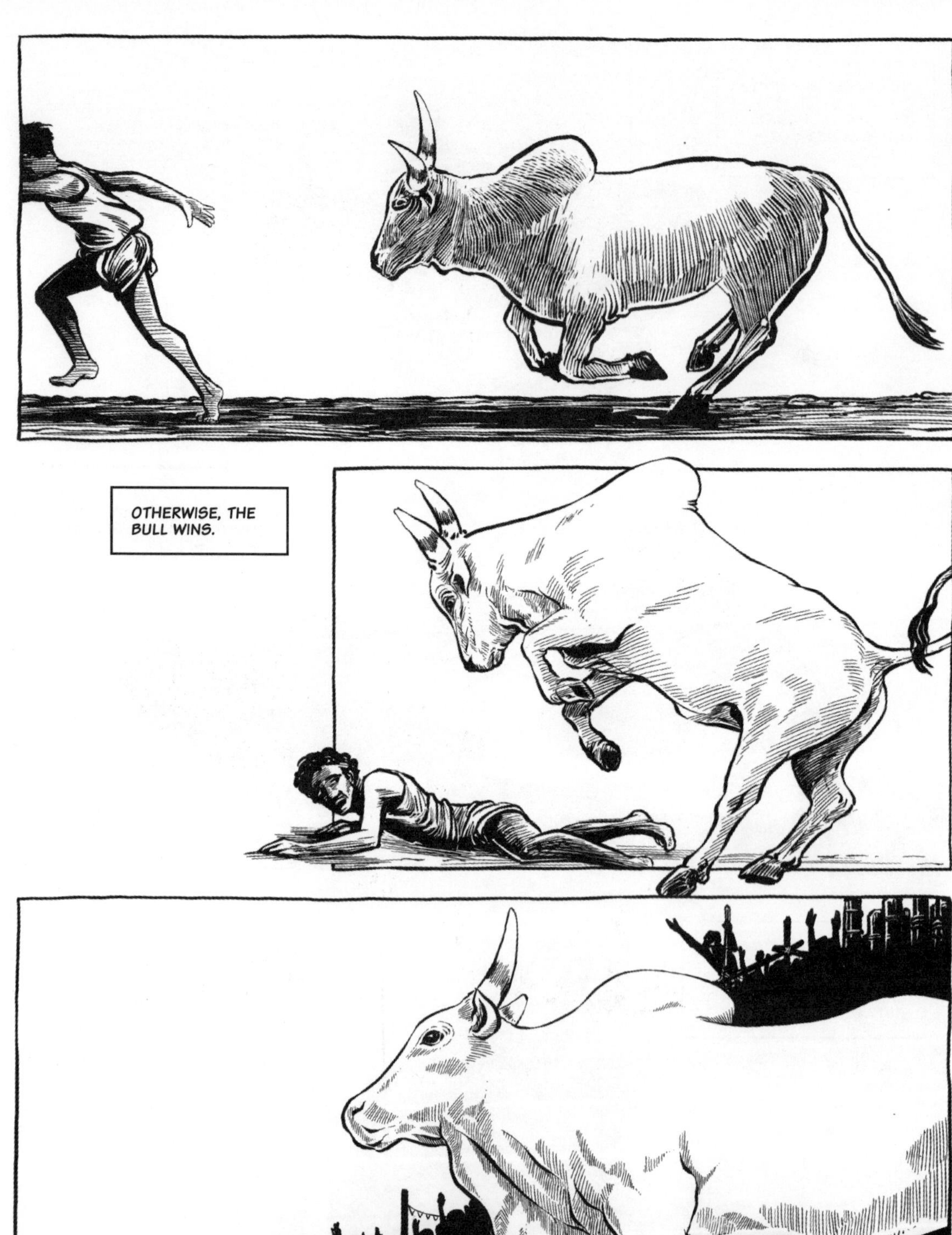
OTHERWISE, THE BULL WINS.

EITHER WAY, FOR EACH AND
EVERY CONTEST THAT EVENING,
MAN OR BULL WILL EMERGE
CHAMPION IN THE VAADIVAASAL.

PICHI AND MARUTHAN STAND AT A VANTAGE POINT NEAR THE SIDE GATE. THEY KEEP A KEEN WATCH ON THE PEOPLE AND THE PARADING BULLS.
WON'T THE VAADIPURAM BULL COME TODAY?

I THINK WE ARE GOING TO BE DISAPPOINTED.

I THINK SO TOO!

THEY ALL SAY THE CHELLAYI JALLIKATTU IS THE BIGGEST IN THE REGION!

PFFT! ALL TALK!

THEY SAID A THOUSAND BULLS WILL POUND THESE GROUNDS TODAY...

YOU SEE THE REAL STORY ONLY WHEN YOU'RE HERE! PAH!

AN OLD MAN LOOKS THEM UP AND DOWN.

WHO ARE YOU BOYS? YOU MUST BE FROM THE EAST.
YES, YOU'RE RIGHT.

AH! I HEARD YOU SAYING THIS AND THAT. AND YOUR FRIEND SAID SOME MORE.
OH, THAT WAS JUST BETWEEN US. JUST TALK.

BUT EVERYONE CAN HEAR YOU. EVEN THIS OLD MAN.

HERE TODAY, IF THE LINE-UP IS EVEN ONE BULL LESS THAN 500...

YOU MAY SPIT ON US LOCALS.

YOU SAID IT, OLD MAN! GOOD ONE!

WE DIDN'T MEAN TO
SOUND ARROGANT, AIYA.
GOOD THAT YOU ADMIT
IT, SON. ANYWAY, TRY
NOT BE LOUDMOUTHS.
YOU MAY ADVISE US,
AIYA. WE ARE LISTENING.

WE HAVE EXCHANGED MANY
WORDS, BUT I HAVEN'T
ASKED ABOUT YOU TWO...

I AM PICHI, AND HE
IS MY BROTHER-IN-
LAW, MARUTHAN.

FROM?

USILANOOR.

USILANOOR?!

USILANOOR OR THE NEIGHBOURHOOD?

USILANOOR ONLY. WHY?

OH! IT IS A PLACE WORTHY OF WORSHIP.

THE SPIRIT AND TRADITION OF JALLIKATTU RUNS DEEP EVEN IN A NEWBORN IN USILANOOR! YOU ARE LUCKY TO HAIL FROM SUCH A PLACE.

BUT WILL YOU GIVE THIS UP FOR THAT? WHAT WE HAVE IS NO GREATER THAN THIS CHELLAYI JALLIKATTU WE SEE HERE.
AAH, BUT THE EASTERN JALLIKATTU IS DIFFERENT.

EY, YOU MENTIONED A VAADIPURAM BULL.

WERE YOU TALKING ABOUT THE KAARI BULL?

YES.
THE ONE ZAMINDAR BOUGHT FOR 2,000 RUPEES FROM THE EAST?

YES. DOESN'T LOOK LIKE IT'S COMING TODAY, IS IT?

HAHA!
HAHA!

A JALLIKATTU WITHOUT THE ZAMINDAR'S BULLS! I HAVE NEVER SEEN SUCH A THING.

THAT'S WHAT WE THOUGHT TOO. WE ARE FIRST-TIMERS HERE.

THOSE BULLS WILL BE COMING. THEY WILL.

LOOK. THOSE ARE THE ZAMINDAR'S PEOPLE— THEY WILL ALL ENTER TOGETHER.

THE ZAMINDAR IS EVERYTHING HERE. LOOK AT THE STAGE.

THE BIG CHAIR IS FOR HIM. THE OTHERS ARE FOR THE SUB-COLLECTOR AND SUPERINTENDENT OF POLICE.

MAKE WAY.

THE PERIYAPATTI BULLS ARE COMING!

THE ZAMINDAR'S BULLS... THEY ARE HERE!

BROTHERS, TAKE A LOOK AT THOSE 20 BULLS, MARCHING IN LIKE LIONS!

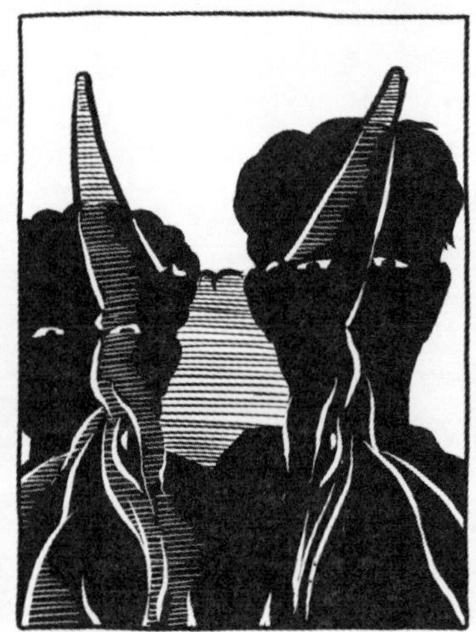

THE DECORATED BULLS ARE WELCOMED INTO THE ARENA.

THE GROUND SHAKES BENEATH THEIR HOOFS. THEY STIR UP CLOUDS OF DUST.

OY BROTHERS!
YES AIYA, GO ON!
SEE THAT ONE—IT'S THE KARAMBAI BULL!

THERE ARE SO MANY BULLS. WHERE IS THAT ONE WE ASKED ABOUT?
THE KAARI? WHY, ARE YOU GOING TO JUMP ON IT?

NO, IT'S THE FAMOUS ONE. WE JUST WANT TO SEE IT.

AH, I SEE, IT'S THE BULL FROM YOUR AREA.

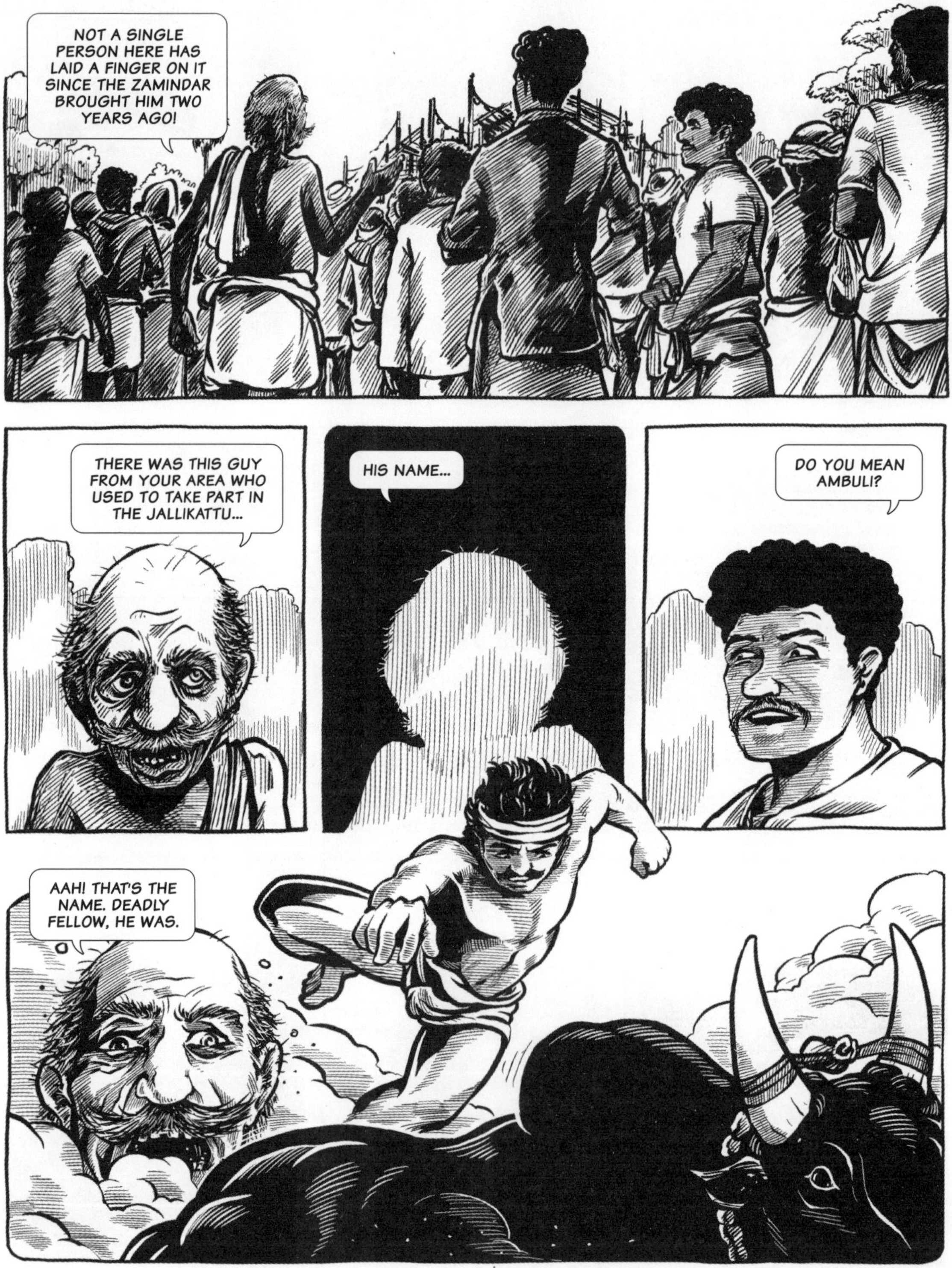

THERE WAS THIS GUY FROM YOUR AREA WHO USED TO TAKE PART IN THE JALLIKATTU...

HIS NAME...

DO YOU MEAN AMBULI?

AAH! THAT'S THE NAME. DEADLY FELLOW, HE WAS.

I HEARD HE DIED FROM INFECTION AFTER THE KAARI GORED HIM.

A LEGEND THAT ENDED THAT DAY.

GRANDPA, THIS BOY IS HIS SON!
OH MY SON... PICHI!

YOU MUST BE BLESSED TO BE BORN OF A FATHER LIKE AMBULI!

THAMBI, NEITHER MAN NOR BULL SHOULD SHED A TEAR IN THE JALLIKATTU.
THAT TOO, ONE WHO HAS AMBULI FOR A FATHER. NO, NO!

COME, SIT WITH ME. LET'S CHEW SOME BETEL LEAVES.

I DID THIS WITH YOUR FATHER LONG AGO...

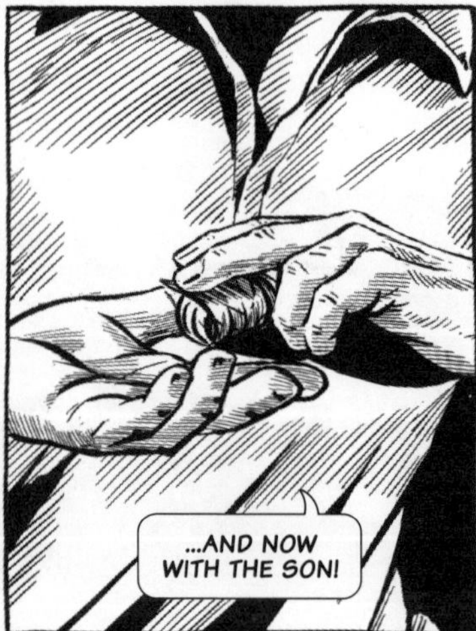
...AND NOW WITH THE SON!

OH AMBULI.

IT WAS AT THE USILANOOR JALLIKATTU TWO YEARS AGO.

AMBULI WAS OVER 40 WHEN HE FACED THE KAARI.

PICHI... WHATEVER HAPPENS, DON'T INTERFERE.

THE SCENE FLASHED IN PICHI'S MIND.

COME ON, IT'S YOUR FATHER'S WISH.

AFTER ME, ALL THE VAADI WILL BELONG TO YOU.

WAIT HERE. THE KAARI IS NOT FOR YOU, SON.

DON'T LET MY BOY INTO THE VAADIVAASAL!

PICHI WATCHED AS HIS FATHER CHARGED INTO THE ARENA FOR THE LAST TIME.

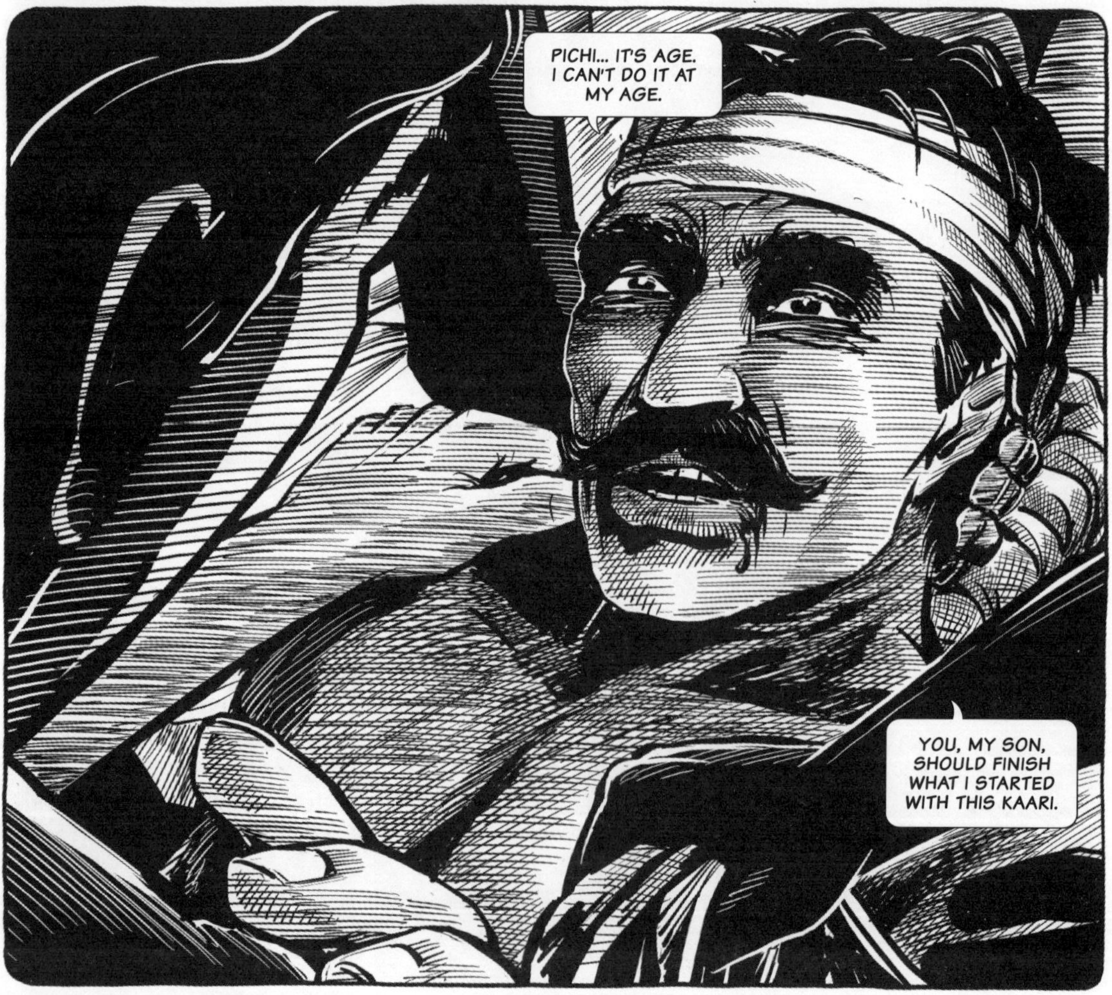

PICHI... IT'S AGE. I CAN'T DO IT AT MY AGE.

YOU, MY SON, SHOULD FINISH WHAT I STARTED WITH THIS KAARI.

OH, HE'S HERE TO PROVE HIMSELF, NO DOUBT.
CAN HE LIVE UP TO HIS LEGACY? HE'S HERE TO SETTLE OLD SCORES.
EASTERN MEN ARE STRONG BULL-CATCHERS.
WILL HE DARE TO CHALLENGE THE ZAMINDAR'S BULL? DOES HE HAVE IT IN HIM?
WORD SPREADS QUICKLY ABOUT PICHI, THE MAN FROM THE EAST.

PICHI IS ALERTED BY THE SOUND OF THE DRUMS.

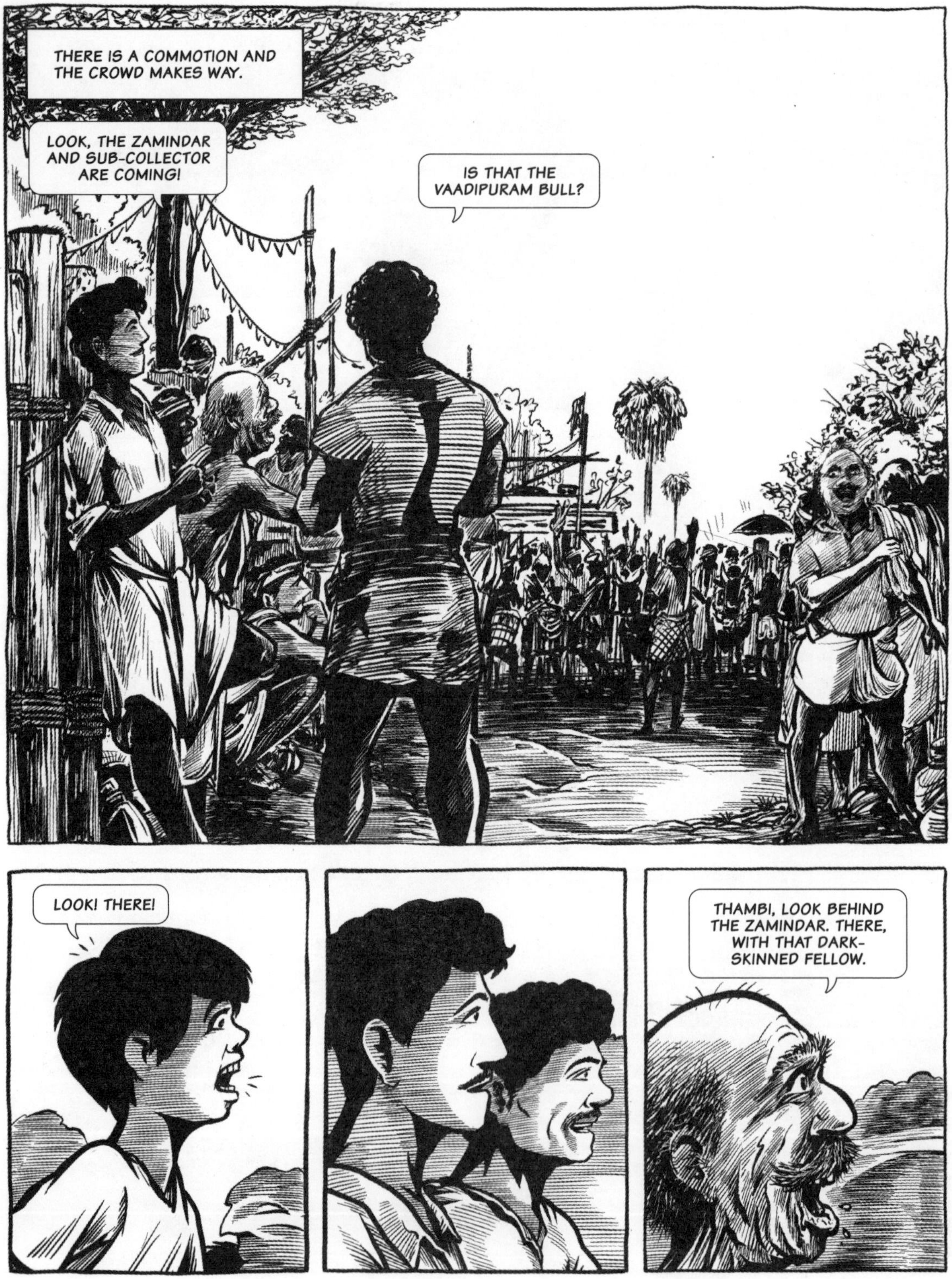

THERE IS A COMMOTION AND THE CROWD MAKES WAY.

LOOK, THE ZAMINDAR AND SUB-COLLECTOR ARE COMING!

IS THAT THE VAADIPURAM BULL?

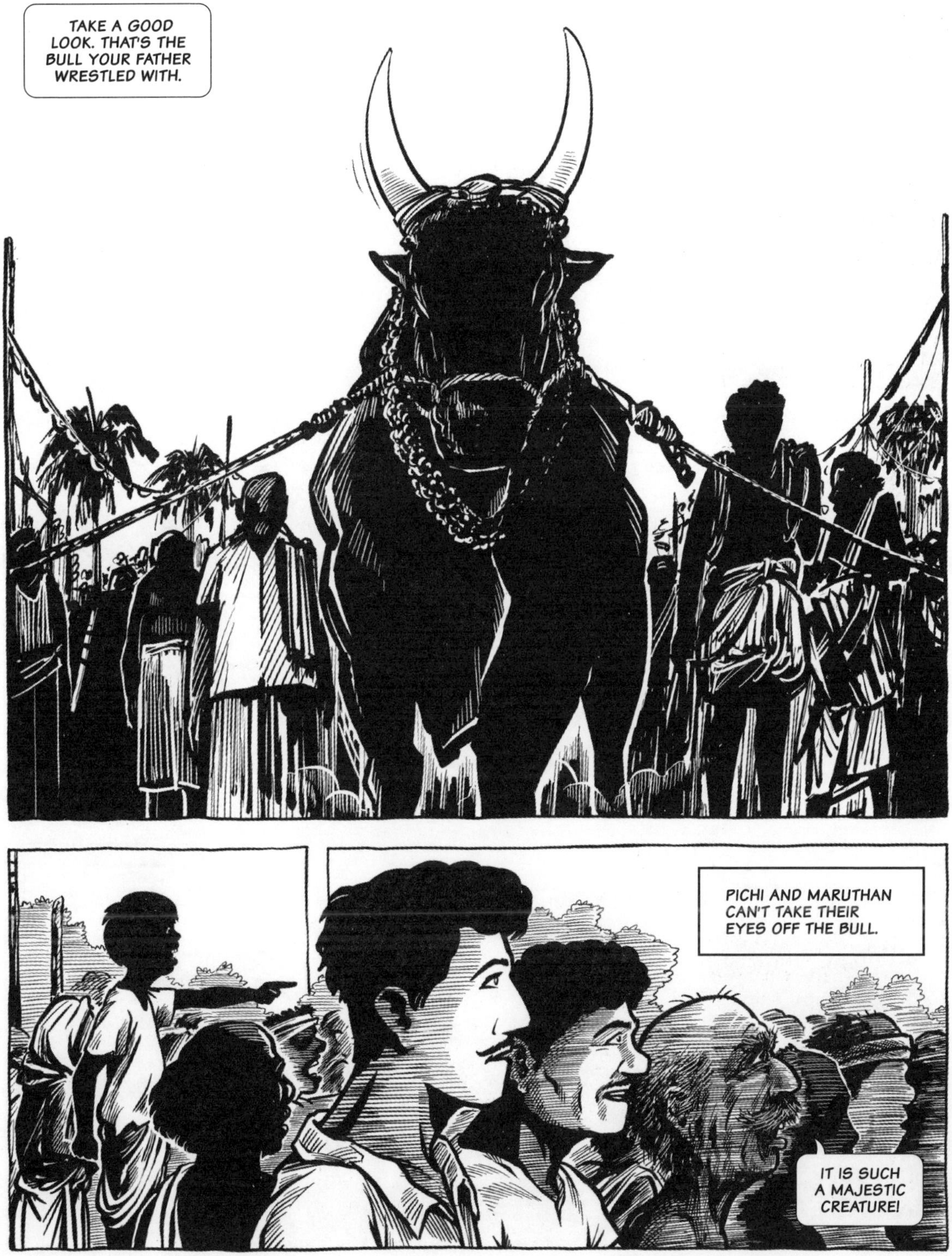

TAKE A GOOD LOOK. THAT'S THE BULL YOUR FATHER WRESTLED WITH.

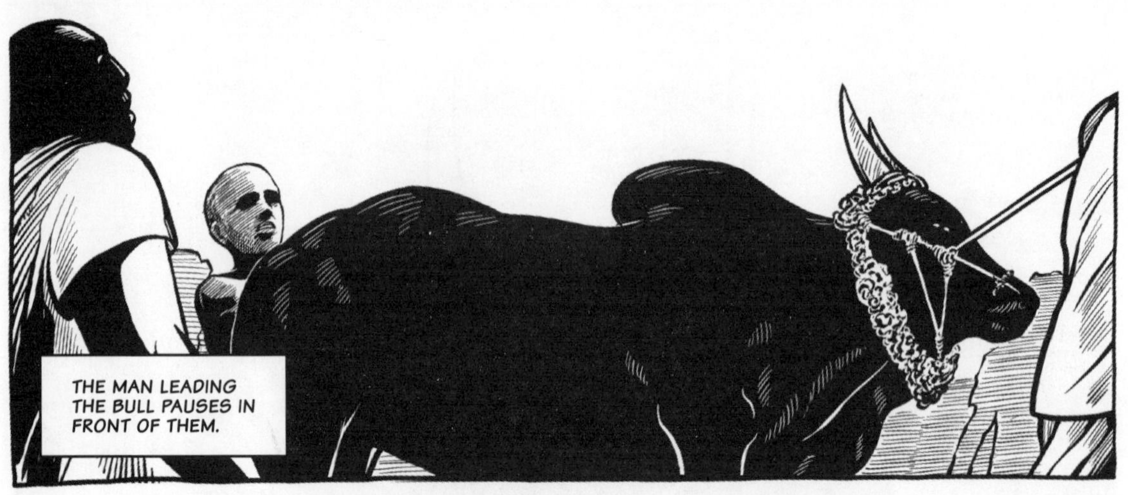
THE MAN LEADING THE BULL PAUSES IN FRONT OF THEM.

PICHI PUSHES THROUGH THE CROWD TO STAND ACROSS IT.
THE BULL AMBLES AROUND, SNIFFING AND SNORTING.

HIS FATHER HAD TOLD HIM ABOUT IT, BEFORE HE DIED.
HE WAS A MAN OF THE SOIL!
PICHI REMEMBERS THOSE HORNS WITH HIS FATHER'S BLOOD ON THEM.

YET, PICHI AND MARUTHAN ARE EQUALLY AWED BY THE KAARI'S POISE AND POWER.

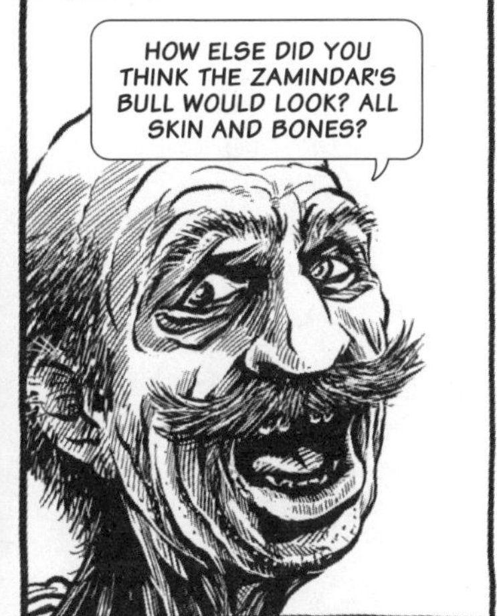
HOW ELSE DID YOU THINK THE ZAMINDAR'S BULL WOULD LOOK? ALL SKIN AND BONES?

PICHI SMILES AND RETURNS HIS GAZE TO THE BULL.
THE CROWD PULLS BACK AS THE KAARI RESUMES ITS MARCH.

THE ZAMINDAR
TURNS TO ADMIRE
THE BULL BRIEFLY.

HE THEN PAUSES TO
GREET THE CROWD
BEFORE ADDRESSING
THEM FROM THE STAGE.

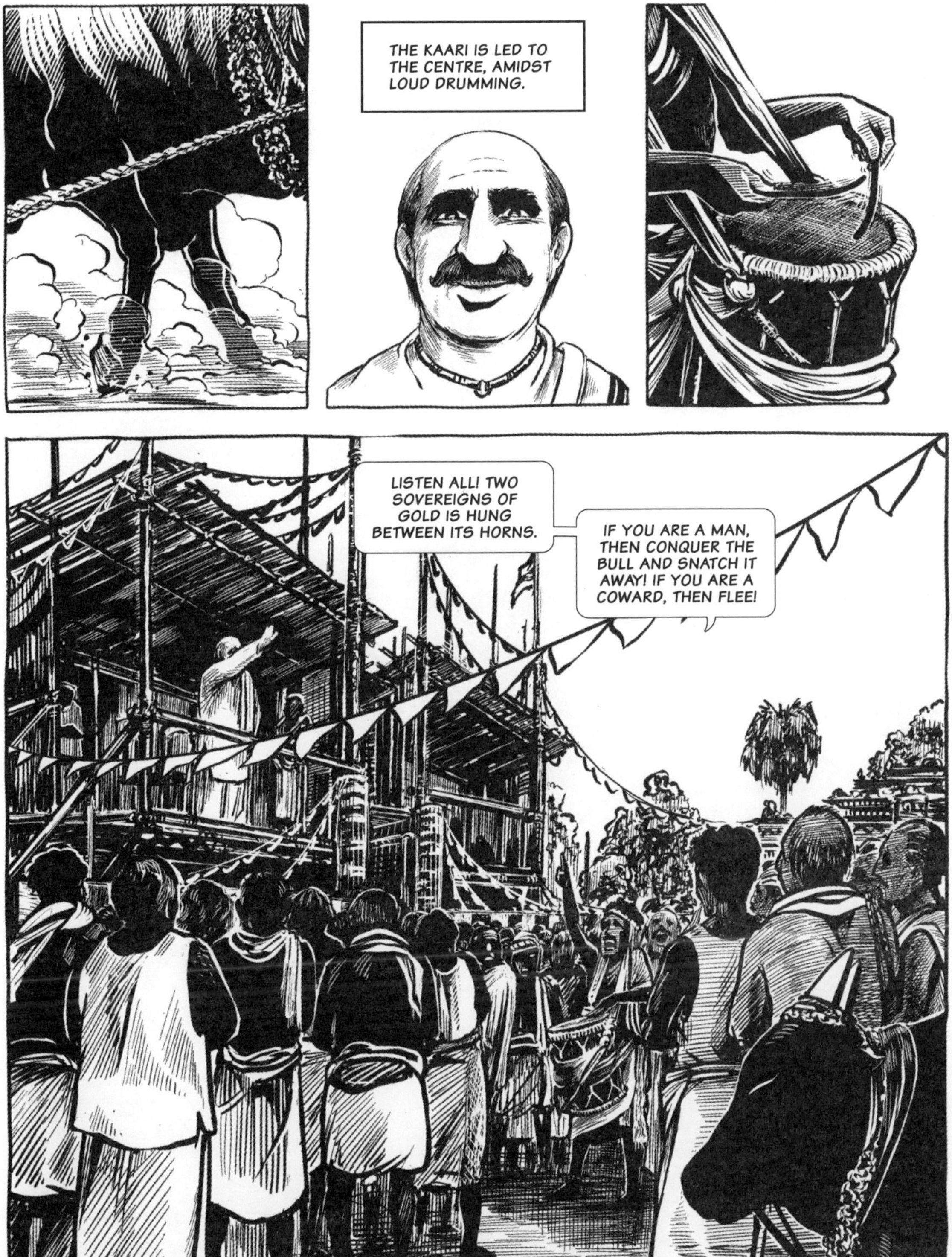

LISTEN ALL! TWO SOVEREIGNS OF GOLD IS HUNG BETWEEN ITS HORNS.

IF YOU ARE A MAN, THEN CONQUER THE BULL AND SNATCH IT AWAY! IF YOU ARE A COWARD, THEN FLEE!

AS THE BULL IS LED TO THE ENCLOSURE, PICHI NOTES THE PRIDE IN THE ZAMINDAR'S EYES.

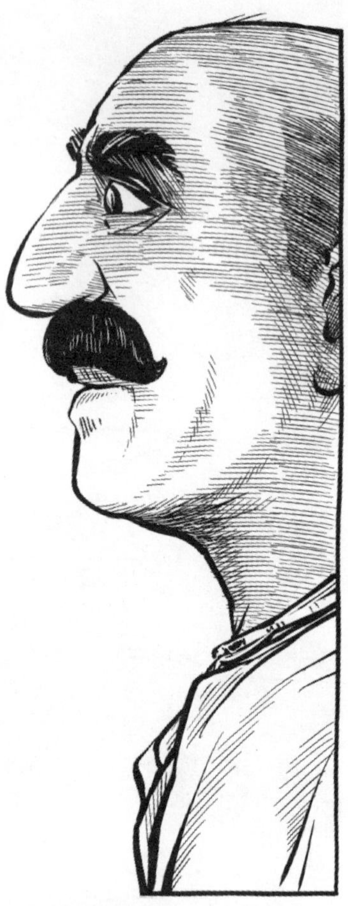

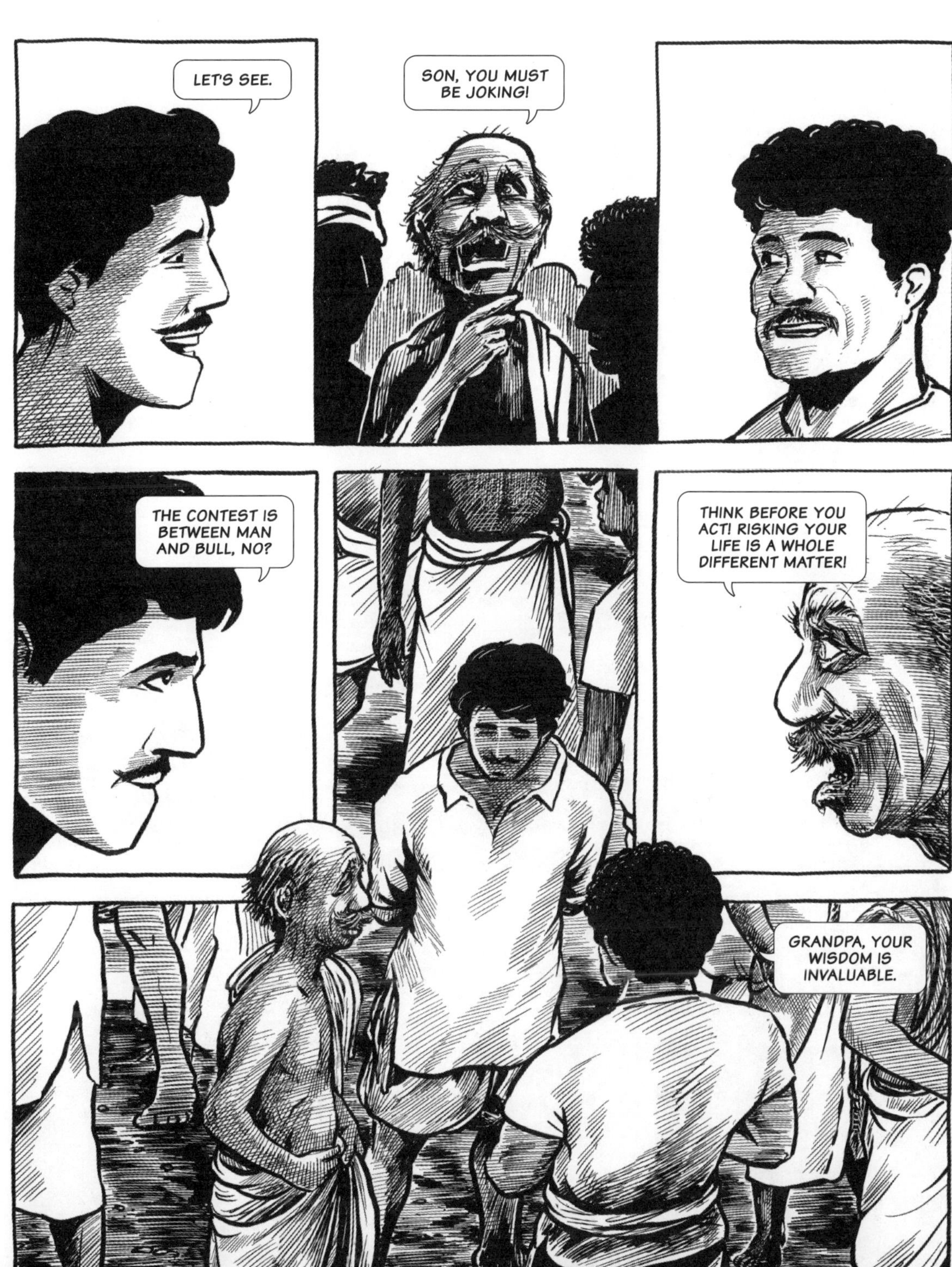
LET'S SEE.
SON, YOU MUST BE JOKING!
THE CONTEST IS BETWEEN MAN AND BULL, NO?
THINK BEFORE YOU ACT! RISKING YOUR LIFE IS A WHOLE DIFFERENT MATTER!
GRANDPA, YOUR WISDOM IS INVALUABLE.

THE CHELLAYI ARENA IS ABUZZ WITH ANTICIPATION.

SHALL WE RELEASE THE BULLS?

THE ZAMINDAR NODS IN AGREEMENT.

THE CHELLAYI TEMPLE BULL IS RELEASED FIRST.

NO ONE MUST CATCH IT.

HOOI...
HOOI!
THE CROWD CHEERS AND MAKES WAY FOR IT.

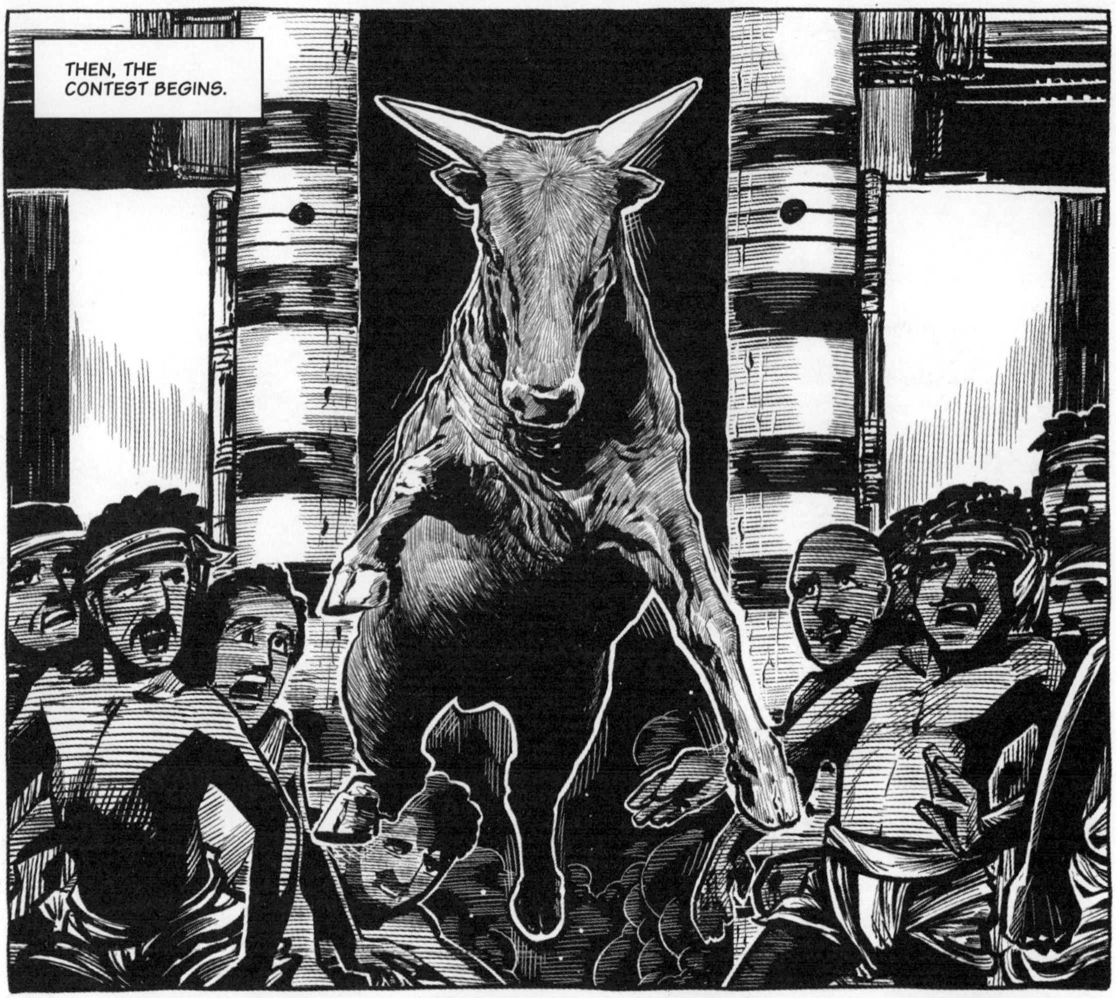

THEN, THE CONTEST BEGINS.

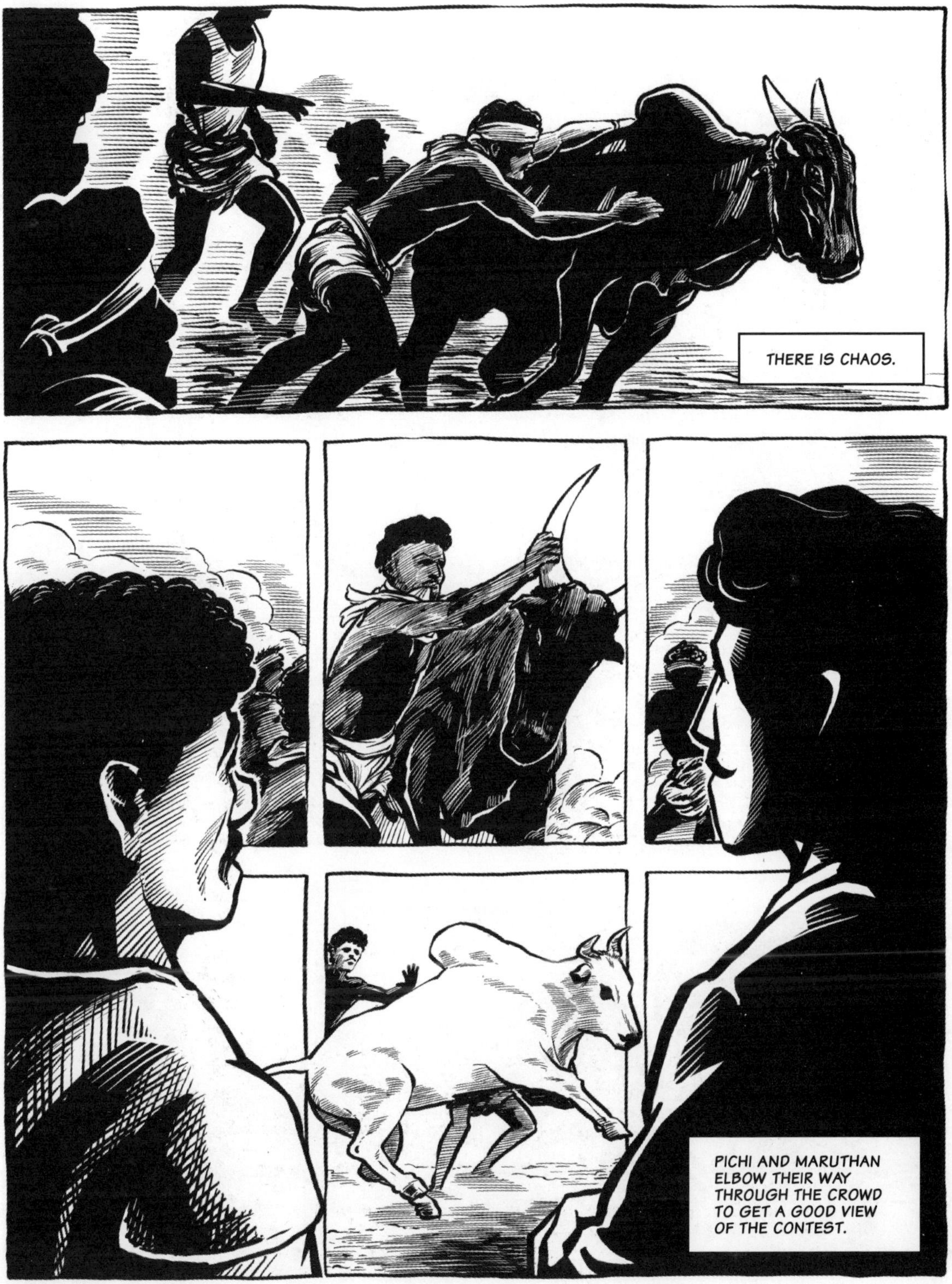

PICHI AND MARUTHAN ELBOW THEIR WAY THROUGH THE CROWD TO GET A GOOD VIEW OF THE CONTEST.

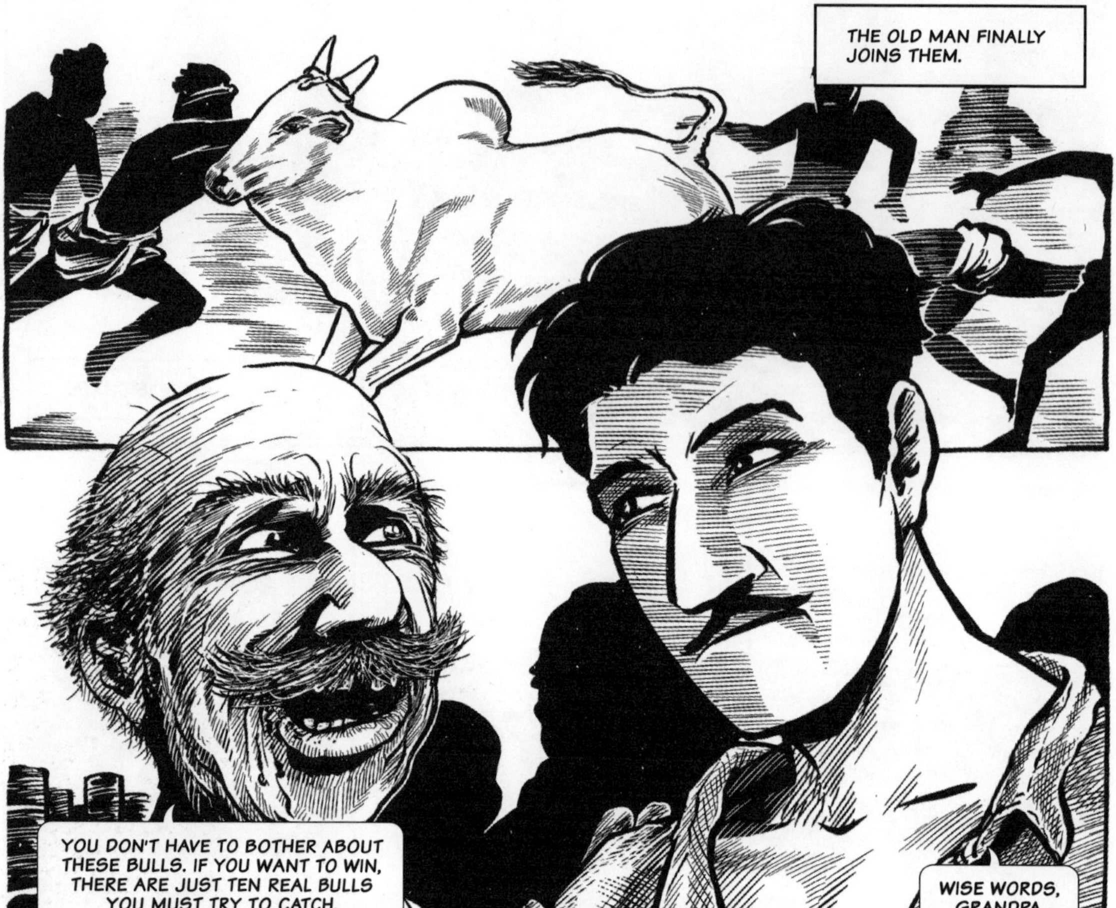

THE OLD MAN FINALLY JOINS THEM.

YOU DON'T HAVE TO BOTHER ABOUT THESE BULLS. IF YOU WANT TO WIN, THERE ARE JUST TEN REAL BULLS YOU MUST TRY TO CATCH.

WISE WORDS, GRANDPA.

AH, THAT IS MURUGU. ALL TALK AND FULL OF HIMSELF!

WE ARE MEETING FOR THE FIRST TIME, MURUGU.
I'VE SEEN YOU BEFORE AT THE JALLIKATTU, WITH YOUR FATHER.

SO, YOU'RE ALSO HERE TO JUST STARE AT THE BULLS, HUH?
HA! WELL SAID, MY BOY!

MURUGU IS INFURIATED WITH THE INSULT.

BUT PICHI GOES ON.
KNOW THIS: A MAN FROM THE EAST DOESN'T COME HERE TO STARE AT THE JALLIKATTU. HE WILL MAKE OTHERS STARE!

ALL I SEE IS AN ASS BOASTING ABOUT HIS FATHER.

LET'S NOT CREATE A SCENE IN THE VAADIVAASAL, BROTHER.

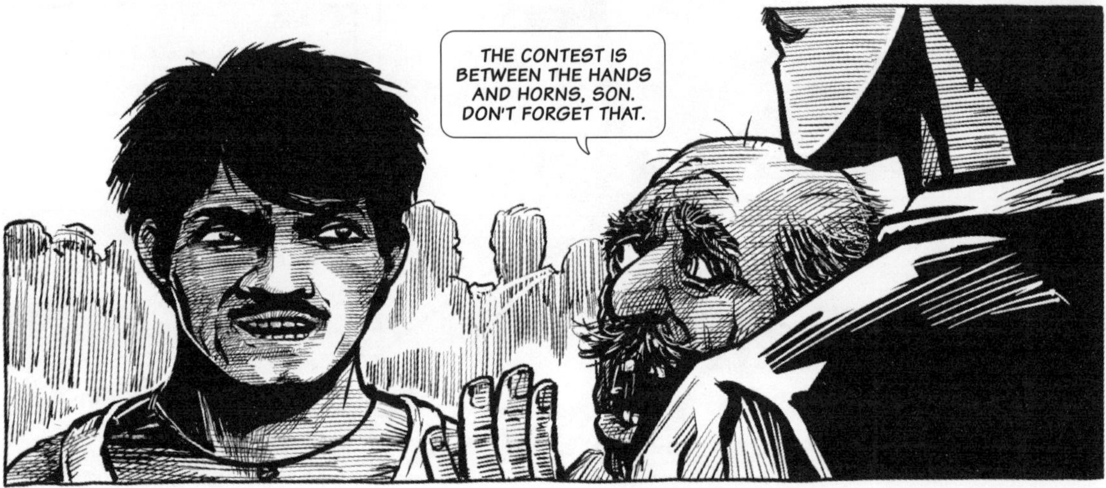
THE CONTEST IS BETWEEN THE HANDS AND HORNS, SON. DON'T FORGET THAT.

WAIT, MURUGU. THE GAME HAS JUST BEGUN!

THE CROWD IS ABUZZ WITH RUMOURS ABOUT THE BOYS FROM THE EAST.

PICHI AND MARUTHAN PREPARE THEMSELVES AND ENTER THE ARENA.

IT'S THE BILLAI BULL

MURUGU, YOU CATCH THIS ONE!

WHAT'S THE HURRY, OLD MAN? TRYING TO PROVOKE ME WHEN THE REAL CHALLENGE IS ONLY COMING?

AT A SIGN FROM PICHI, MARUTHAN MOVES IN.

AT THE SAME TIME, MURUGU MAKES A CHARGE FOR THE BULL.

THE OLD MAN HOLDS BACK MARUTHAN, TO LET MURUGU TRY.

WHEN THE BULL SLIPS FROM MURUGU,
THE OLD MAN TAUNTS HIM.

YOU THINK IT'S GOING TO OFFER ITS HORNS FOR YOU TO HOLD?
WHAT ARE YOU DOING BROTHER? PRUNING SPINACH?
SUDDENLY, PICHI LEAPS IN...

...AND TAKES CHARGE OF THE BULL IN NO TIME.

HERE, MURUGU! TAKE YOUR REWARD—IT'S BETWEEN THE HORNS!

COME ON, GET IT. DON'T YOU WANT IT?

OK, GO!
PICHI PUSHES THE BULLS HORNS AWAY FROM HIM AND JUMPS BACK.

THE CROWD IS ECSTATIC.
HE CAUGHT THE BULL!
LOOK AT MURUGU'S FACE!

HE'S ONLY GOOD FOR THE PLOUGH NOW!

HOW WILL YOU FACE YOUR ZAMINDAR NOW, MURUGU?

PICHI, WHAT YOU DID IS NOT RIGHT!

HOW CAN YOU CALL HIM AND OFFER THE REWARD FROM YOUR BULL!

THAT WASN'T MY BULL, GRANDPA!

IT WAS HIS.

THE BULLS
KEEP COMING.

THE CONTEST
GOES ON.

AS PICHI RETREATS
TO WATCH THE
ACTION, A SILK HEAD
CLOTH FALLS ON HIM.

PICHI!

PICHI! THE ZAMINDAR IS CALLING YOU!

THE ZAMINDAR IS CALLING!

PICHI GREETS THE ZAMINDAR RESPECTFULLY WITH A SMILE.
HE GIFTS PICHI A FIVE-RUPEE NOTE.

GO ON, YOU CATCH THE BULLS WELL! YOU'RE FROM USILANOOR?

YES, SIR. AS YOU SAY, SIR.

THE OLD MAN COLLECTS PICHI'S WINNINGS.
CLEVER BOY!

THE KORAAL BULL IS COMING!

MARUTHAA!

PICHI AND MARUTHAN ADVANCE AS OTHERS RETREAT AT THE SIGHT OF THE BULL.

THE KORAAL HAS SMALL HORNS.

MARUTHAN FAILS TO HOLD ON TO THEM.

PICHI SKILFULLY TAPS THE BULL'S LEG...

...CAUSING IT TO STUMBLE AND FALL.

HE QUICKLY GRABS ITS HORNS AND SNATCHES THE REWARD.

THE BULL GETS UP ENRAGED, AND CHARGES INTO THE CROWD.

THE CROWD LIFTS UP PICHI. HE IS GREETED BY MORE ADMIRERS AND REWARDS.
IT MUST BE CASTRATED AND SENT TO THE FIELDS NOW!
HA! THE KORAAL DROPS ITS DUNG AND FLEES!
IT'S NOT EVEN WORTH THAT!

THE ZAMINDAR CALLS HIM AGAIN.

THIS TIME HE IS GIFTED A TEN-RUPEE NOTE.

PICHI FEELS AWKWARD BEING CARRIED BY THE CROWD.

ARE YOU EYEING THE KAARI?

NOTHING LIKE THAT, SIR. IT DEPENDS...
ALRIGHT, RESUME THE GAME!

REMEMBER, SIR...

...THERE WAS A MAN WHO DIED TRYING TO CATCH THE KAARI IN THE USILANOOR JALLIKATTU?
THIS IS HIS SON. HE HAS COME TO CATCH THE KAARI HERE.
YES. HE HAS ALREADY BARED HIS HEART TO ME.

SON, DID YOU SEE THE ZAMINDAR'S EXPRESSION? THE KAARI BULL MEANS EVERYTHING TO HIM!
YES, IT'S ALL OVER HIS FACE.

I WON'T TELL YOU WHAT YOU ALREADY KNOW ABOUT THE KAARI.

MAY CHELLAYI AATHA PROTECT YOU!

OYEE! THE KAARI BULL IS HERE!

THE BLACK DEVIL!
IT'S A MONSTER!

THE CROWD DISPERSES, LEAVING ONLY A FEW PLAYERS IN THE ARENA.

THE MAN FROM THE EAST IS GOING TO CATCH THE KAARI!
NAH. HE'S GOING TO DIE!
THIS CHELLAYI JALLIKATTU WILL BE HIS LAST!

THE KAARI IS LIKE THE DIVINE NANDI TO THE ZAMINDAR.
POOR BOY.

PICHI ACKNOWLEDGES THE ZAMINDAR'S GAZE.

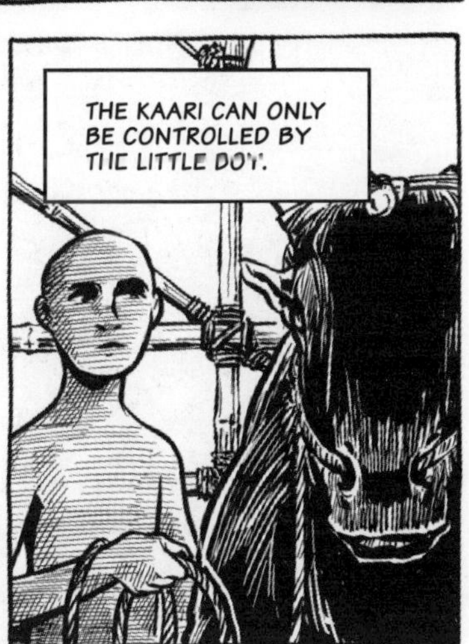
THE KAARI CAN ONLY BE CONTROLLED BY THE LITTLE BOY.

IT'S NOT AN EASY BULL TO DECIPHER.
READY!

THAT PICHI IS RETREATING. JUST A SHOW-OFF FROM THE EAST!

THAT BOY IS DONE FOR.
STOP BLABBERING. LOOK AT HIM. CATCHING BULLS RUNS IN HIS BLOOD.

THE LITTLE BOY UNTIES THE KAARI'S NOOSE AND RUNS OUT OF THE VAADIVAASAL .

THE CROWD FALLS
SILENT AS THE
KAARI EMERGES.

IT IS INDEED A
TOUGH BULL.
A MONSTER!

WILL IT BE THE
BEAST OR THE MAN
FROM THE EAST?

MURUGU SNEAKS UP BEHIND THE BULL AND LETS OUT A CALL.

THE BULL STANDS STILL AS LONG AS PICHI AND MARUTHAN DON'T MAKE A MOVE.

AS THE KAARI SPINS TOWARDS PICHI, HE STANDS MOTIONLESS.

LOOK AT IT! IS IT A BULL OR A MAN?

THE CROWD STARTS CHEERING SOFTLY.
THE BULL STANDS ROOTED, BREATHING HEAVILY AND STAMPING.

ON PICHI'S SIGNAL...

...MARUTHAN RAISES A CALL.
DURRRREEE!

HE DIVES IN AND FLICKS THE BULL'S TAIL.

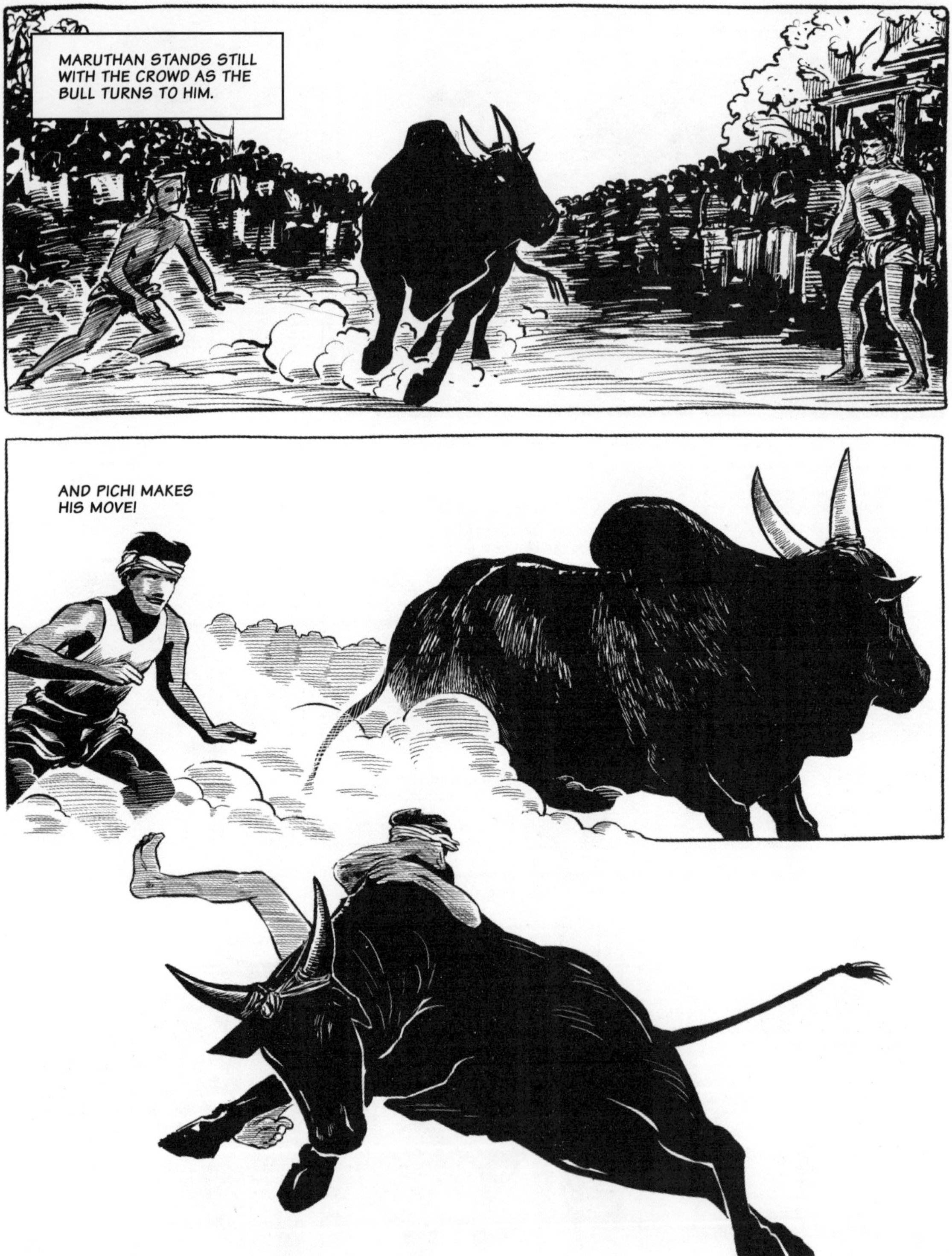

AND PICHI MAKES HIS MOVE!

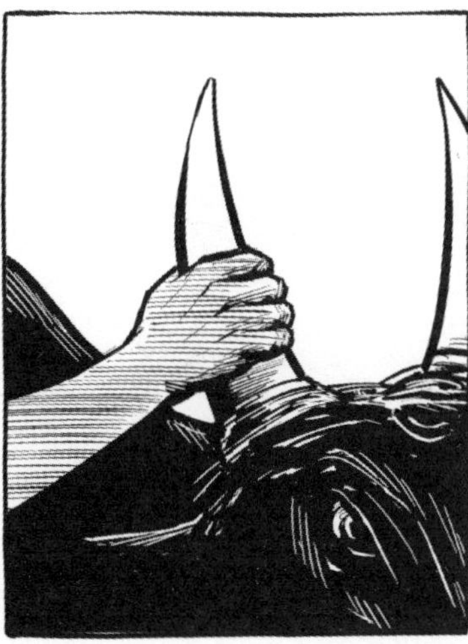

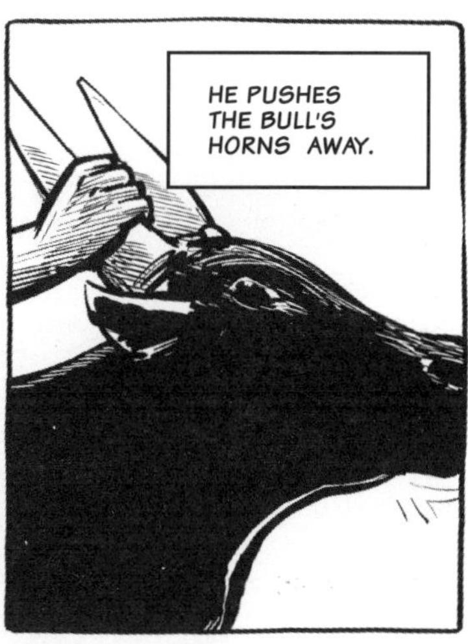

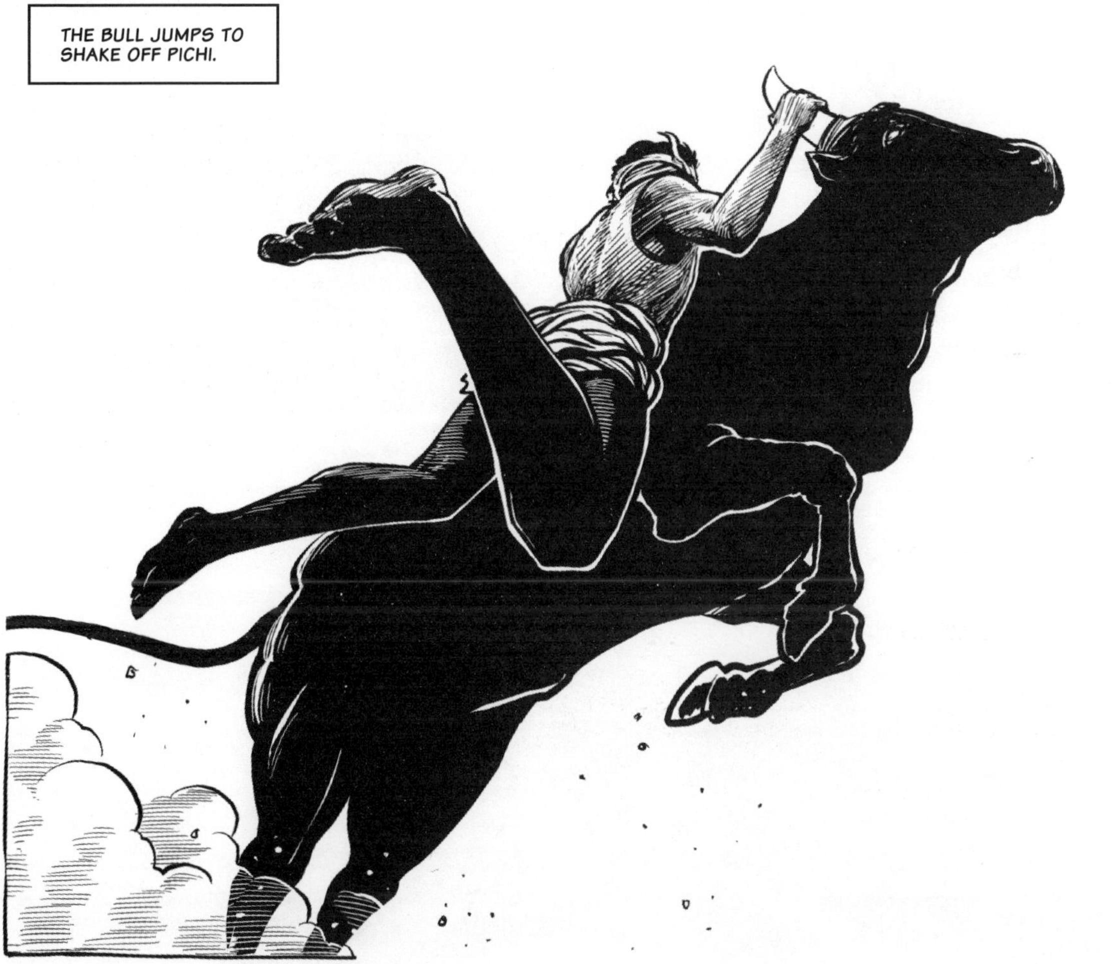

THE BULL JUMPS TO SHAKE OFF PICHI.

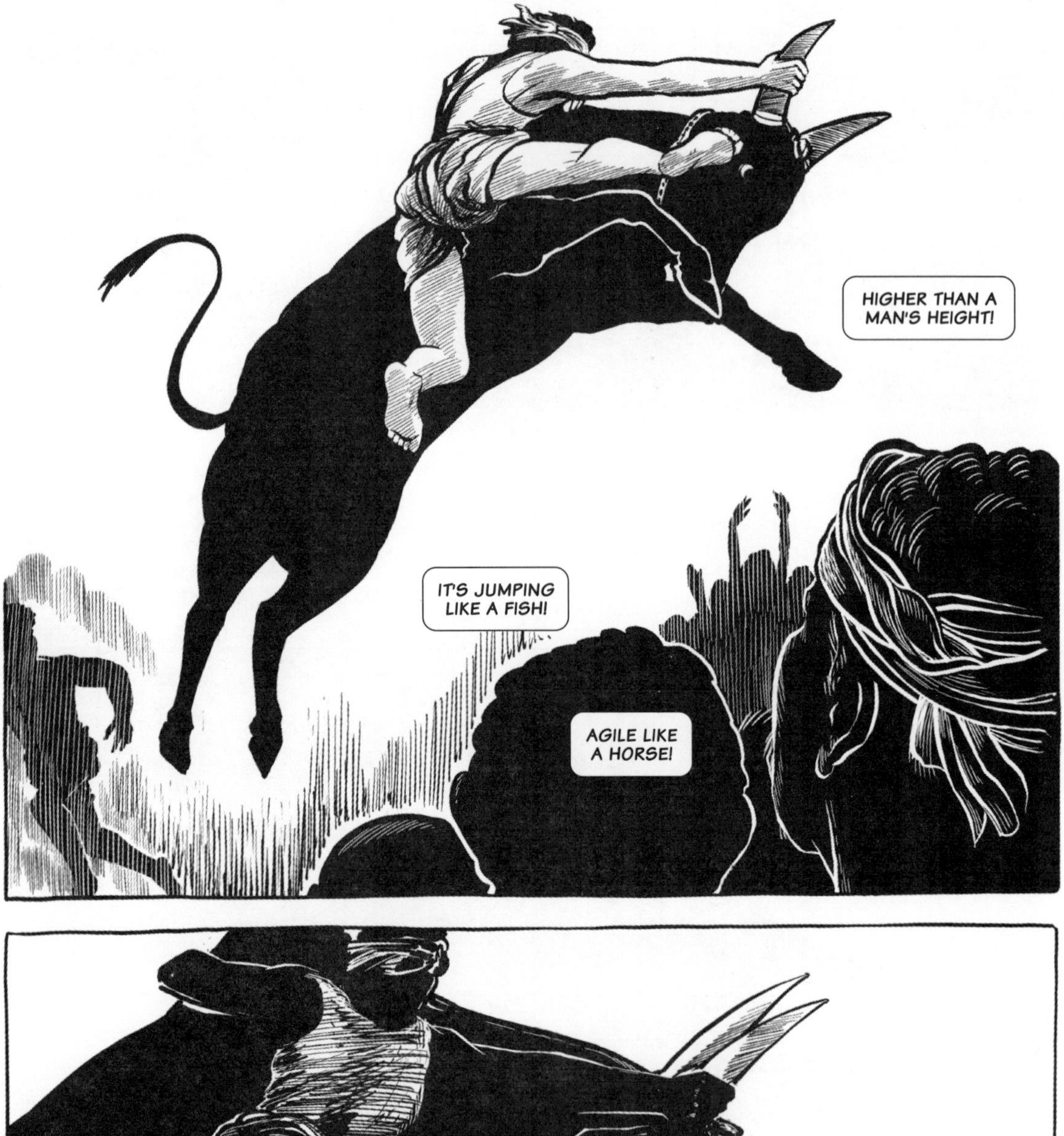

HIGHER THAN A MAN'S HEIGHT!

IT'S JUMPING LIKE A FISH!

AGILE LIKE A HORSE!

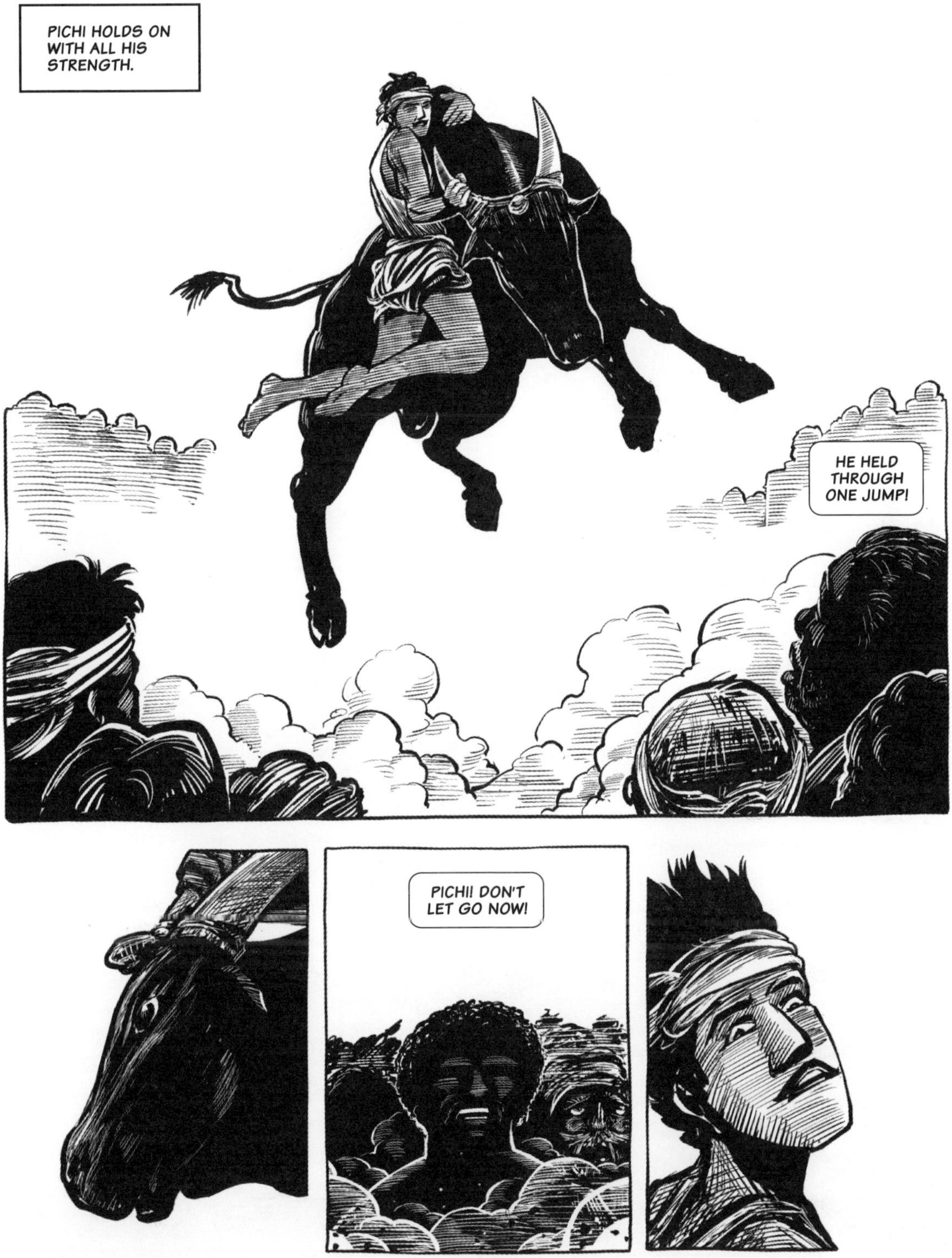

PICHI HOLDS ON WITH ALL HIS STRENGTH.

HE HELD THROUGH ONE JUMP!

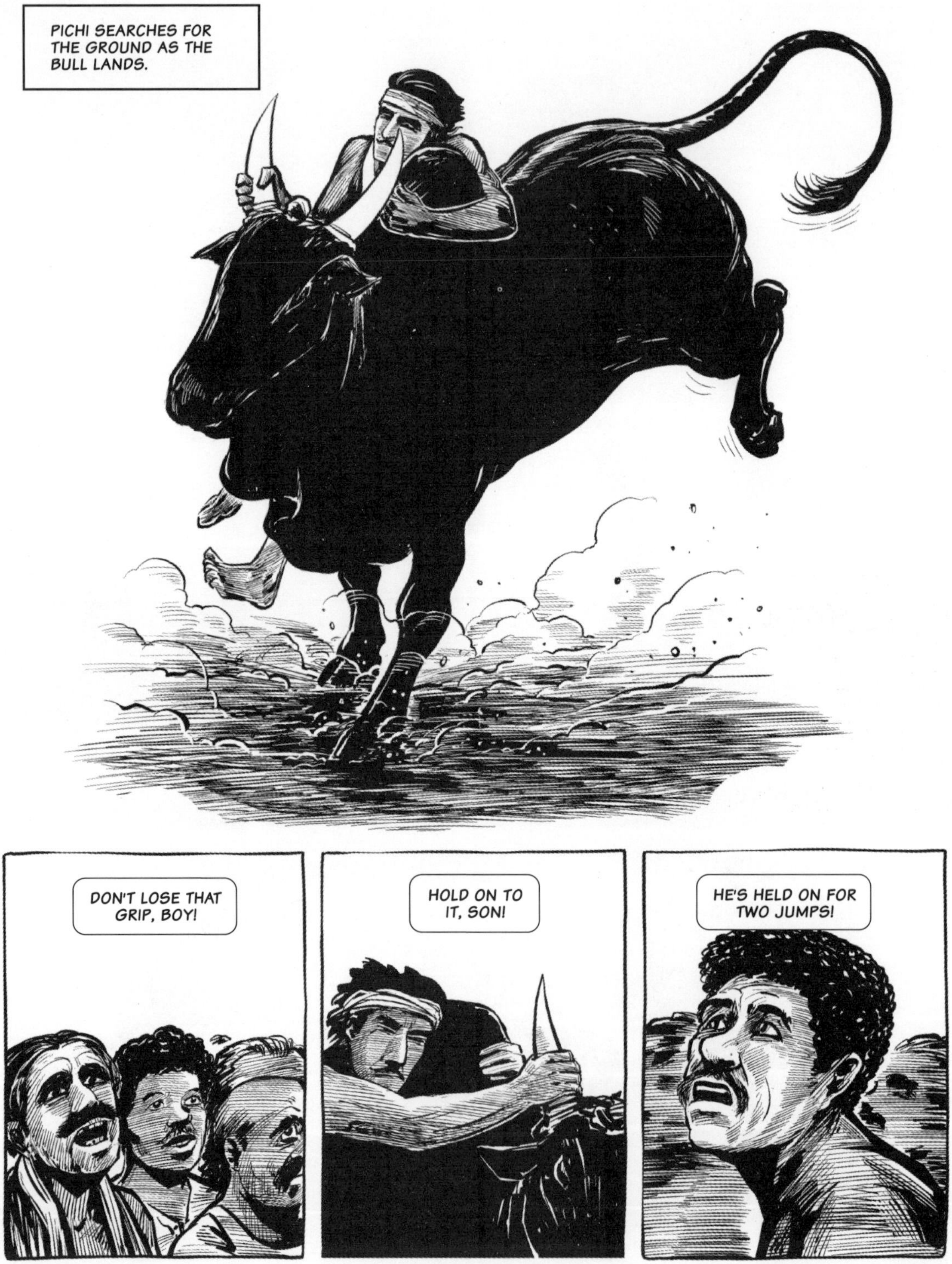

PICHI SEARCHES FOR THE GROUND AS THE BULL LANDS.

BEFORE PICHI CAN STEADY HIMSELF, THE BULL LAUNCHES ITSELF AGAIN.
THE BULL IS TIRED! THE THIRD LEAP IS NOT HIGH!

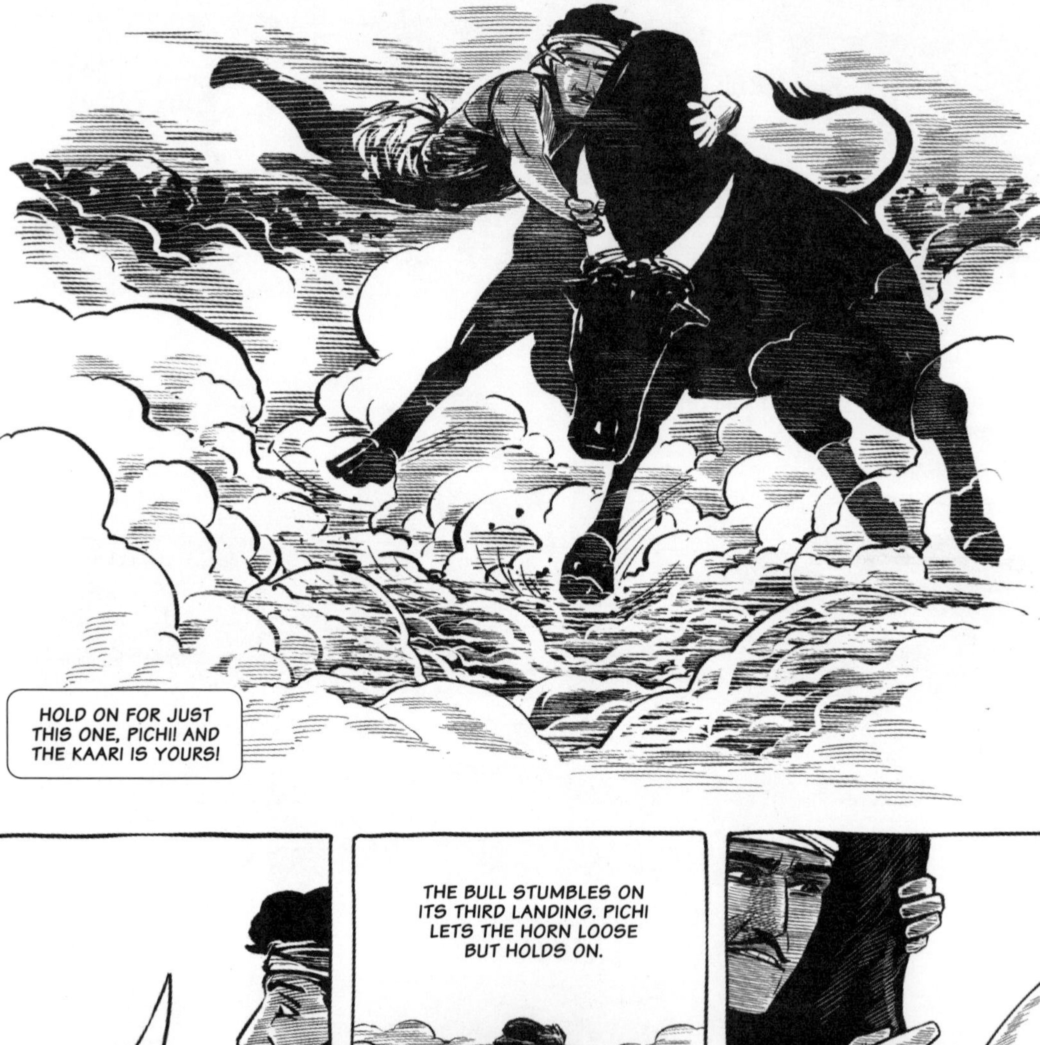

HOLD ON FOR JUST
THIS ONE, PICHI! AND
THE KAARI IS YOURS!

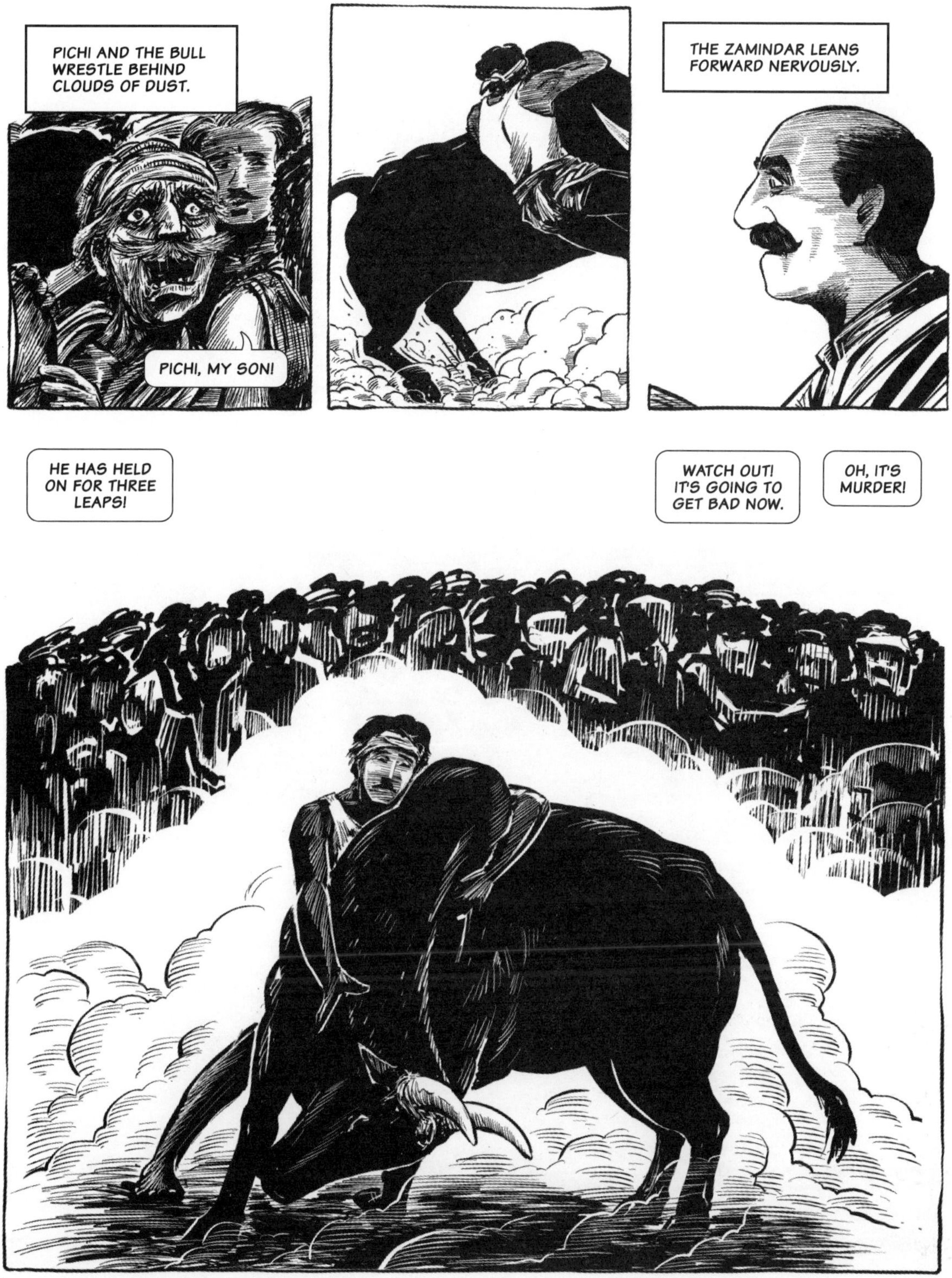

PICHI AND THE BULL WRESTLE BEHIND CLOUDS OF DUST.

PICHI, MY SON!

HE HAS HELD ON FOR THREE LEAPS!

WATCH OUT! IT'S GOING TO GET BAD NOW.

OH, IT'S MURDER!

AS THE KAARI SWERVES TO STRIKE PICHI, HE GRABS THE HORN AGAIN.

THIS TIME, THE BULL STARTS SPINNING.

WHAT A CREATURE!
IT'S SPINNING LIKE A WHEEL!

HOLD ON, PICHI—THE
DONKEY IS TIRED.

THE BULL SLOWS
DOWN TO A PAUSE.

IT RAISES ITS HEAD AND
BREATHES HEAVILY.

PICHI SEIZES
THE CHANCE...

...TO GET A FIRM GRIP
ON BOTH HORNS.

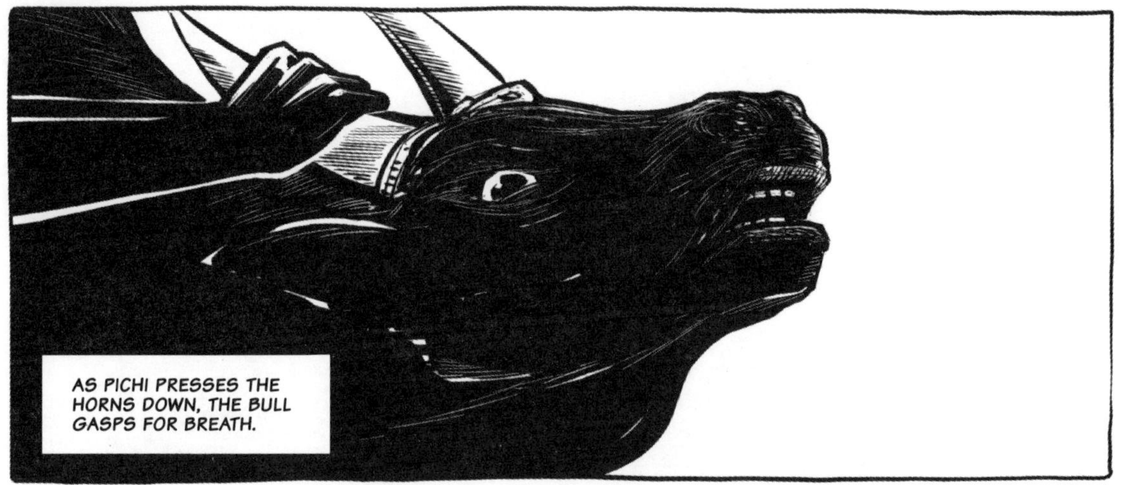
AS PICHI PRESSES THE HORNS DOWN, THE BULL GASPS FOR BREATH.

THE KAARI'S MOUTH HAS BEEN OPENED!
THE MAN FROM THE EAST HAS WON.
LOOK AT THE BULL, LIKE A PUPPY WITH ITS TAIL BETWEEN ITS LEGS!

WITH THE BULL
UNDER CONTROL,
PICHI REACHES
FOR THE PRIZE...

...AND PULLS IT LOOSE.

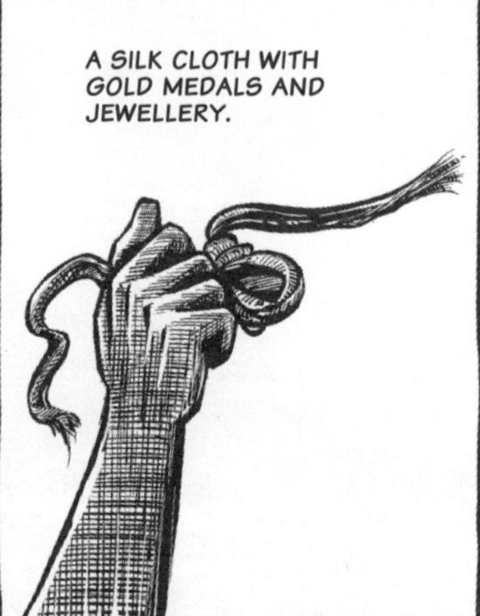
A SILK CLOTH WITH
GOLD MEDALS AND
JEWELLERY.

HE PUSHES THE
BULL AWAY AND
JUMPS BACKWARD.

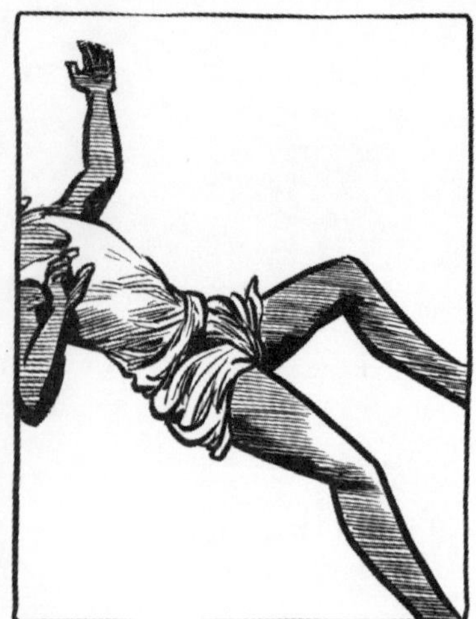
THE JUMP IS MISJUDGED, AND PICHI LOSES HIS BALANCE.
HIS PRIZE FALLS AND SCATTERS.

THE BULL IS COMING BACK! SOMEBODY CHASE THE BULL AWAY!

MARUTHAN TRIES TO INTERVENE AND DISTRACT THE BULL.

BUT IT CHARGES STRAIGHT FOR PICHI.

DURREE DURREE! HOI!

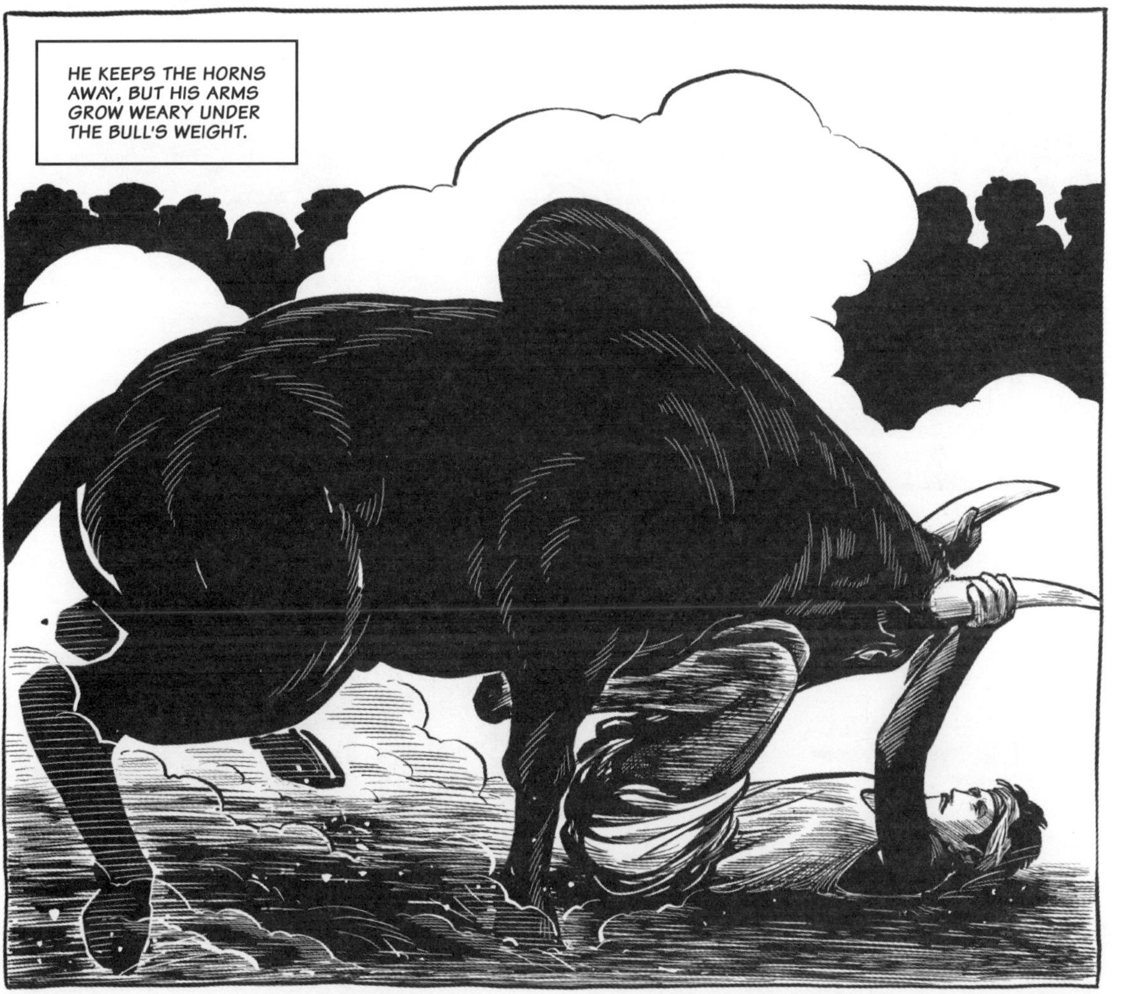

HE KEEPS THE HORNS AWAY, BUT HIS ARMS GROW WEARY UNDER THE BULL'S WEIGHT.

THE BULL PUSHES ON, DRAGGING HIM ALONG THE GROUND.

SOMEBODY, GO CHASE THE BULL AWAY!

MARUTHAA!

TO SAVE PICHI, MARUTHAN IGNORES THE RULES AND PULLS THE BULL'S TAIL.

BUT BEFORE HE CAN STAND UP, THE BULL SWINGS BACK AND STRIKES PICHI.

WITH PICHI DOWN, THE
BULL TRAINS ITS RAGE
ON MARUTHAN.

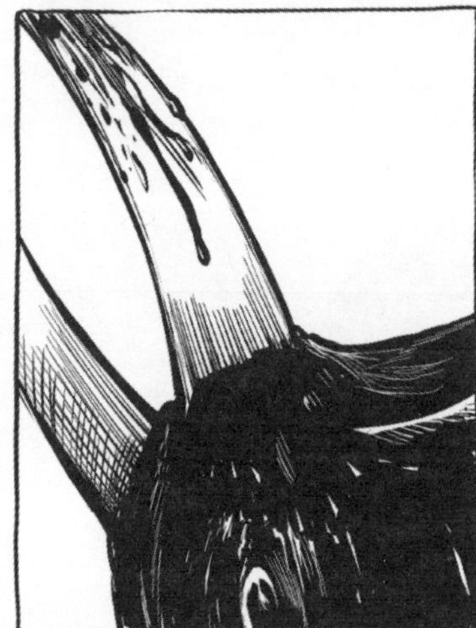

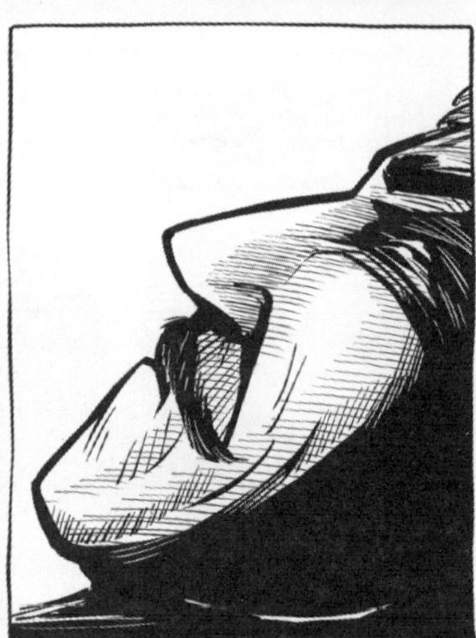

IT SPINS AROUND FIVE
OR SIX TIMES, TRYING TO
SHAKE OFF MARUTHAN.

PEOPLE RUSH IN
AND TEND TO PICHI.

THE KAARI ROCKS BACK AND FORTH IN A FIT OF RAGE BEFORE SLICING THROUGH THE PANIC-STRICKEN CROWD.

TAKE HIM! TAKE HIM
TO THE HOSPITAL!

PICHI IS OUT OF DANGER,
BUT HIS EYES KEEP
SEARCHING.

I'M HERE, PICHI!

YOU'VE DONE IT!
YOU'VE SAVED YOUR
FATHER'S HONOUR!
YES. MY
FATHER'S HEART
WILL BE PROUD.

THAT'S ENOUGH FOR YOUR LIFE, BROTHER.
FOR AN ENTIRE GENERATION!
WHERE'S THE...

WHERE'S THE SILK? THE MEDALS?

HERE IT IS. HERE IT IS.

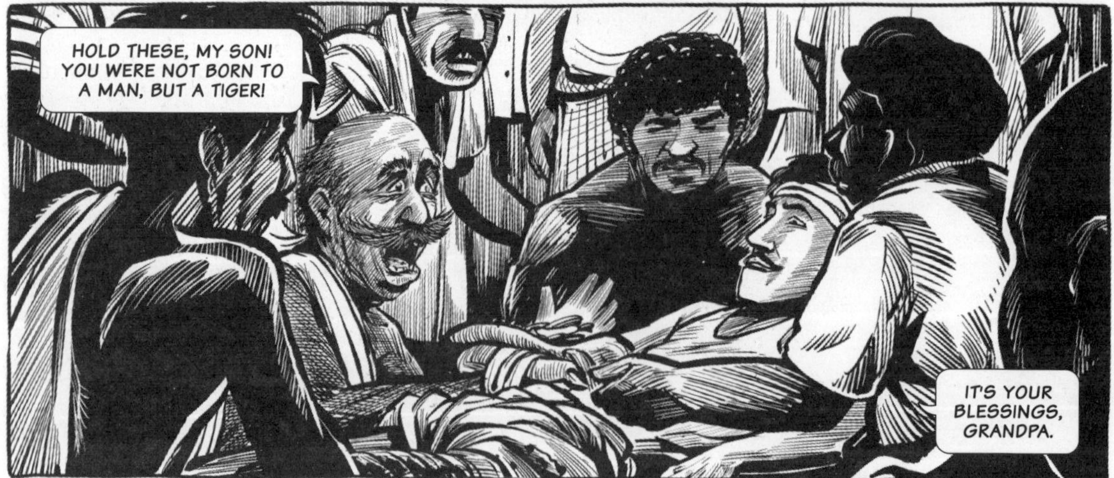
HOLD THESE, MY SON! YOU WERE NOT BORN TO A MAN, BUT A TIGER!
IT'S YOUR BLESSINGS, GRANDPA.

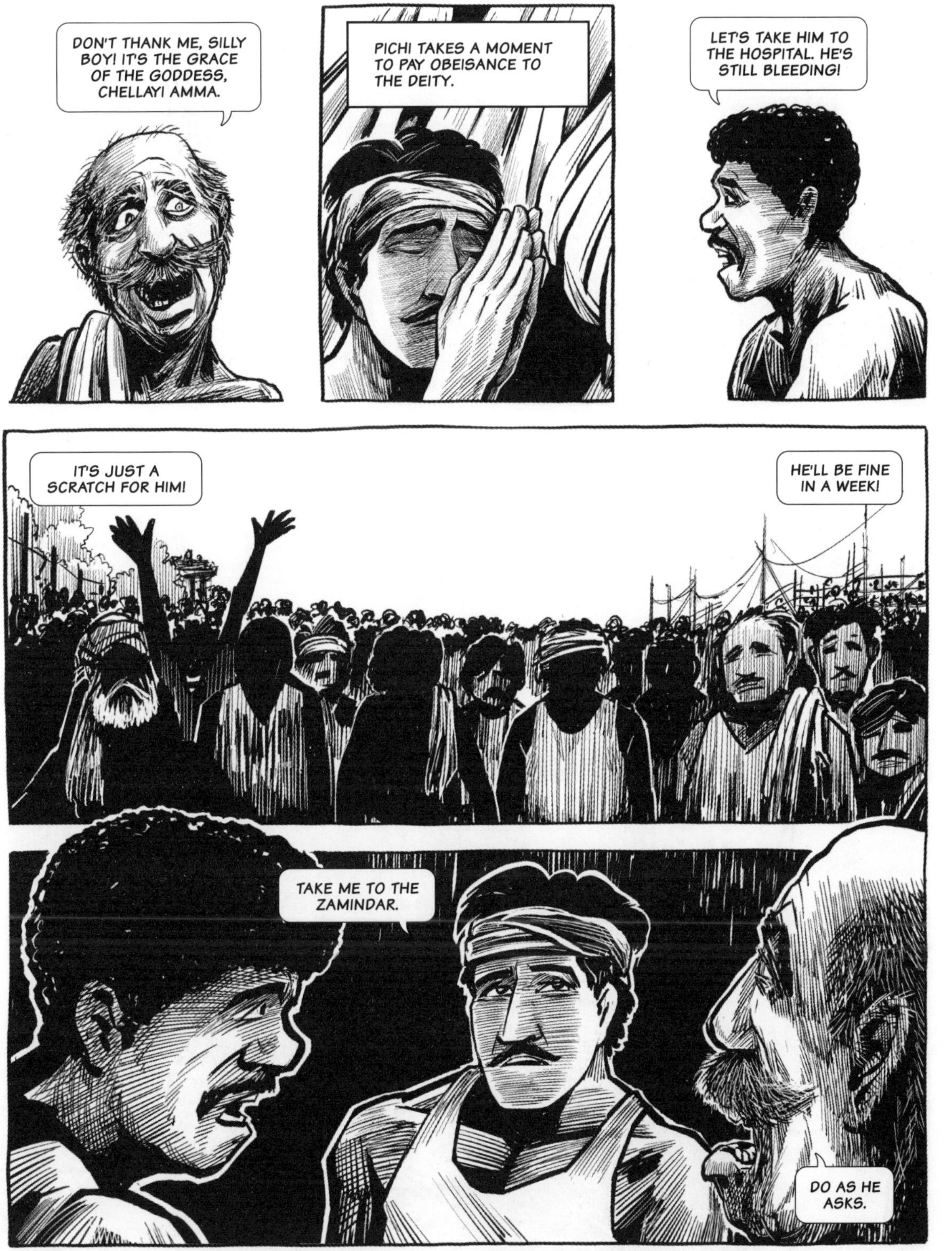

IT'S JUST A SCRATCH FOR HIM!

HE'LL BE FINE IN A WEEK!

TAKE ME TO THE ZAMINDAR.

DO AS HE ASKS.

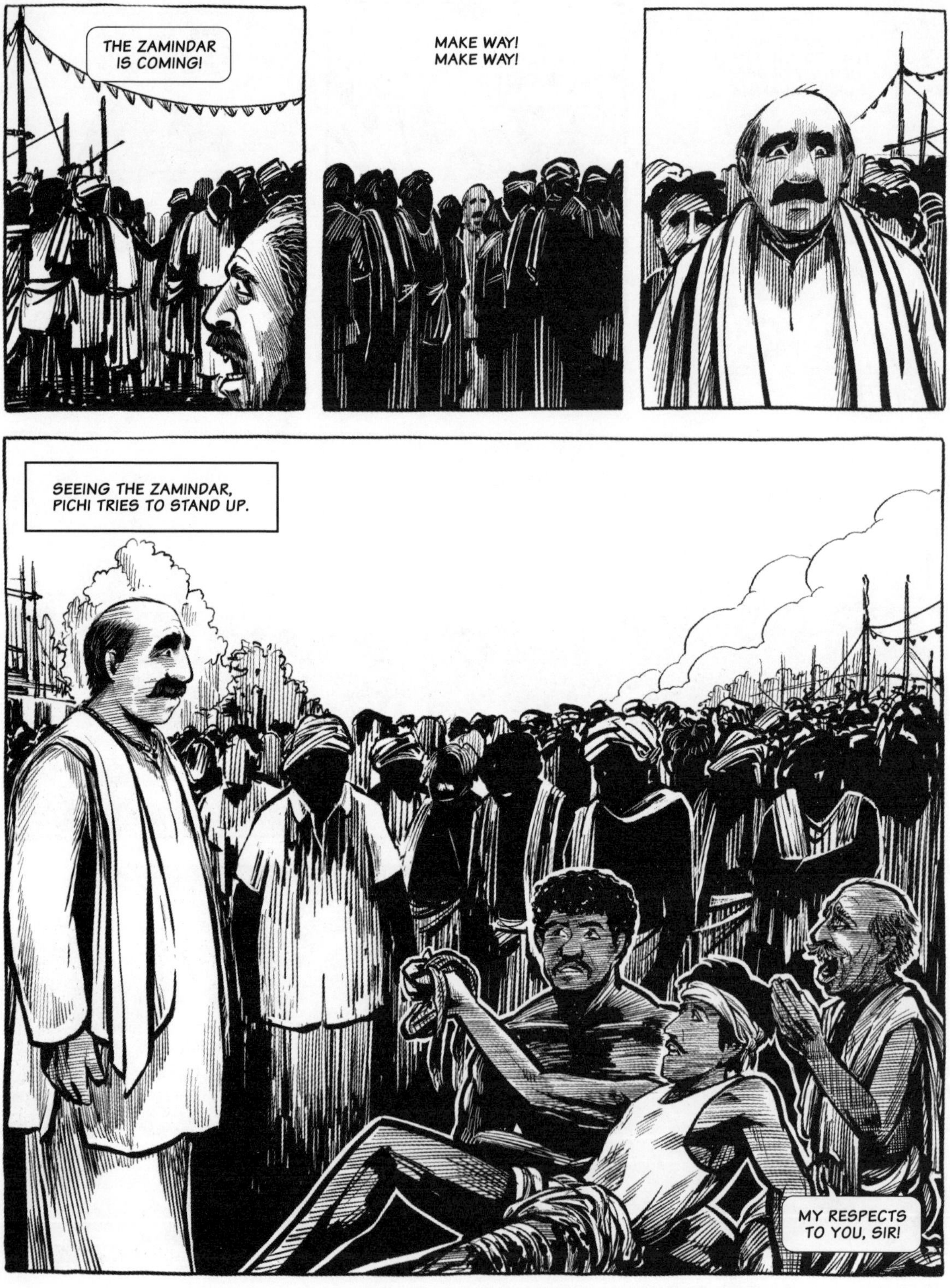

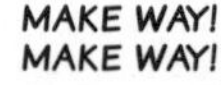

SEEING THE ZAMINDAR,
PICHI TRIES TO STAND UP.

MY RESPECTS
TO YOU, SIR!

THE ZAMINDAR SEES THAT PICHI IS STILL BLEEDING.

HE CONVEYS HIS ADMIRATION WITH A REWARD OF HUNDRED RUPEES AND A SILK HEADSCARF.

PICHI IS TONGUE-TIED, THOUGH HE HAS MUCH TO EXPRESS.

I'M NOT HERE FOR YOUR BULL, SIR! BEFORE MY FATHER DIED, HE SAID, 'THIS KAARI BULL, YOU SHOULD AT LEAST...'
BUT PICHI COULDN'T FINISH HIS WORDS.

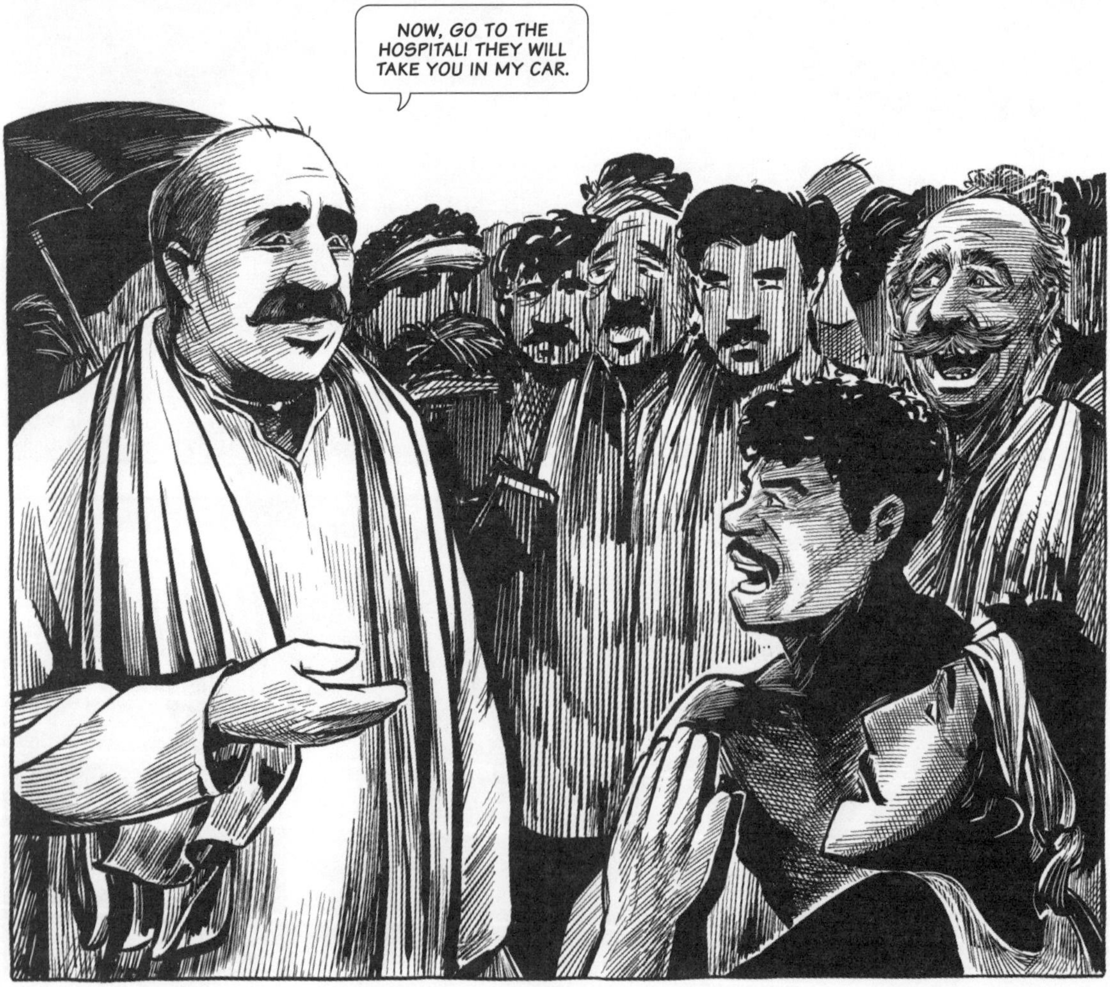

NOW, GO TO THE HOSPITAL! THEY WILL TAKE YOU IN MY CAR.

THE ZAMINDAR WATCHES THE CROWD CHEERING PICHI AS HE IS CARRIED AWAY.

THE KAARI IS FINISHED!
THE EASTERNER HAS PUT THE BULL IN ITS PLACE!
THE KAARI BIT THE DUST!

WHERE IS THE BULL?
IT'S ON THE RIVER BANK, SIR! IT WENT BERSERK AND INJURED TEN PEOPLE HERE.
TWO OF THEM DIED ON THE SPOT.

IT'S STILL MAD. IT WON'T EVEN LET THAT BOY GET CLOSE.

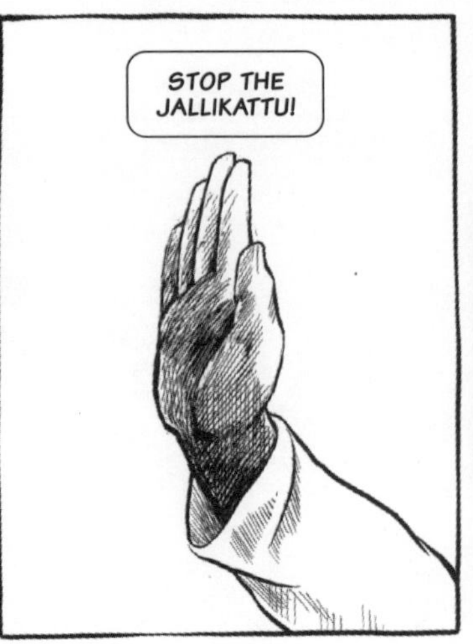
STOP THE JALLIKATTU!

LET'S GO.

THE CROWD FOLLOWS THE ZAMINDAR TO THE SANDY RIVERBED.

THE BULL STANDS,
KICKING AND RAKING
UP A SANDSTORM.

YOU'RE STILL NOT
DONE BEING MAD,
ARE YOU?

THE ZAMINDAR REACHES FOR THE HOLSTER TIED AROUND HIS WAIST.

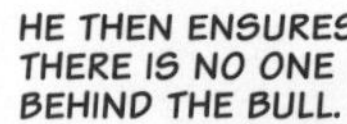

THE ZAMINDAR FIRES
TWO SHOTS.

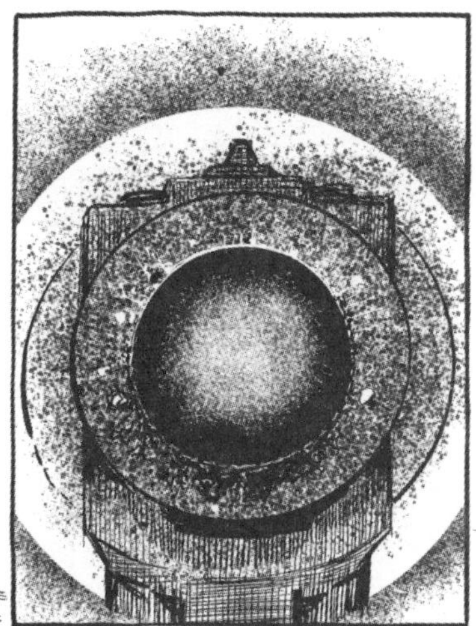

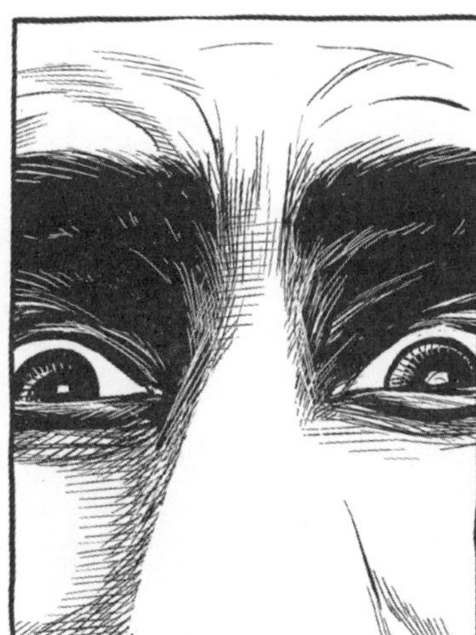

THE KAARI BULL IS DEAD!

THE ZAMINDAR SHOT IT DOWN!

LET'S HEAD BACK.

IT'S OVER IF AN
ANIMAL'S PRIDE
IS HURT.
IT'S OVER EVEN
IF A MAN'S
PRIDE IS HURT.

AFTER ALL, IT IS AN ANIMAL.

Perumal Murugan, principal of Anna College in Namakkal, Tamil Nadu, is the author of twelve novels, five collections of short stories, poems and a memoir, besides ten other books of non-fiction. His novel *Seasons of the Palm* was shortlisted for the Kiriyama Prize in 2005. He won the ILF Samanvay Bhasha Samman in 2015. Murugan's novels *One Part Woman* and *The Story of a Goat* were longlisted for the National Book Award for Translated Literature in 2018 and 2020, respectively. He won the JCB Prize for Literature for *Fire Bird* in 2023. His novel *Pyre* was the first Tamil work to be nominated for the International Booker Prize in 2023.

Appupen is an Indian graphic novelist, writer and artist.
He has published several books and comics like *Moonward* (2009) and *Aspyrus* (2014) that explore an original mythical realm called Halahala.
Appupen's latest graphic novel, *Dream Machine* (2023), deals with the advent of AI and is available worldwide in English, French and German. His socio-political satire, *Rashtraman*, and *Dystopian Times* are regular on various print and online platforms. @appupen is the founder and co-editor of Brainded India.
www.halahala.in

C.S. Chellappa (1912-1998) was a versatile literary personality of his time. His was a varied and wide contribution to different branches of literature, including the novel, short story, poetry, literary criticism and translation, spread over a period of more than five decades.
Chellappa's singular achievement was *Ezhuthu*, a literary magazine that he founded in 1959. In the ten years of its existence, *Ezhuthu* emerged as a seminal force in Tamil literature and has continued to influence literary initiatives in Tamil for the last half a century. With practically no funding from external sources, Chellappa managed to bring out the magazine for over a decade despite severe economic hardships, marking a rare, selfless commitment to the cause of modernising Tamil literature. The author was posthumously awarded by the Sahitya Akademi in 2001.

About Jallikattu

Eru Thazhuvuthal (embracing the bull), also known as *Jallikattu*, is a traditional and heroic sport in Tamil society. It involves humans facing a bull with horns as sharp as swords and attempting to subdue it. A key rule of the sport prohibits spilling the bull's blood on the field.

References to Jallikattu can be found in Sangam literature (written between 300 BCE and 300 CE), as well as in historical inscriptions and Nadukal (hero stones—memorial stones erected in honor of deceased warriors, in this case, sportspersons who lost their lives trying to subdue a bull. The stone typically bears inscriptions of both the human and the bull). The sport continues to thrive in Tamil Nadu to this day.

C.S. Chellappa's novel *Vaadivasal* is set against this backdrop, portraying the grandeur of heroism while delving into the rivalry, jealousy, and malice among participants. The novel also subtly explores the workings of human ego within the context of the game. Written with vivid scenes, *Vaadivasal* offers an engaging and thought-provoking read.

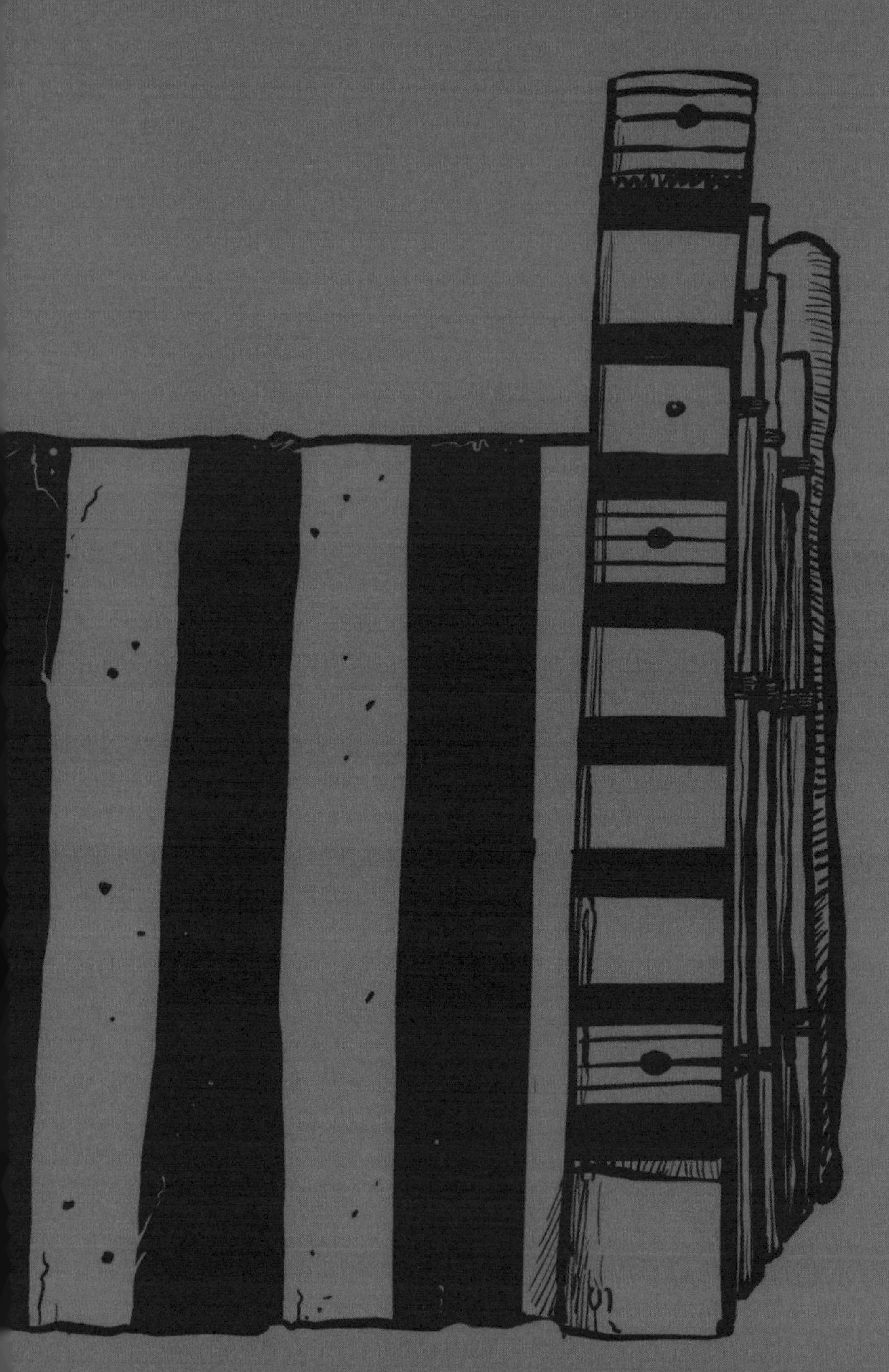